SILAS MARNER

By
George Eliot

SCHOOL OF TOMORROW®

Lewisville, Texas

ISBN 1-56265-021-1

2 3 4 5   Printing/Year   97 96 95

Printed in the United States of America

PART I

Chapter 1

In the days when the spinning wheels hummed busily in the farmhouses—and even great ladies, clothed in silk and thread lace, had their toy spinning wheels of polished oak—there might be seen in districts far away among the lanes, or deep in the bosom of the hills, certain pallid, undersized men, who, by the side of the brawny country folk, looked like the remnants of a disinherited race. The shepherd's dog barked fiercely when one of these alien-looking men appeared on the upland, dark against the early winter sunset; for what dog likes a figure bent under a heavy bag?—and these pale men rarely stirred abroad without that mysterious burden. The shepherd himself, though he had good reason to believe that the bag held nothing but flaxen thread, or else the long rolls of strong linen spun from that thread, was not quite sure that this trade of weaving, indispensable though it was, could be carried on entirely without the help of the Evil One. In that far-off time, superstition clung easily round every person or thing that was at all unwonted, or even intermittent and occasional, like the visits of the peddler or the knife grinder. No one knew where wandering men had their homes or their origin; and how was a man to be explained unless you at least knew somebody who knew his father and mother?

To the peasants of old times, the world outside their own direct experience was a region of vagueness and mystery. To their untraveled thought, a state of wandering was a conception as dim as the winter life of the swallows that came back with the spring; and even a settler, if he came from distant parts, hardly ever ceased to be viewed with a remnant of distrust, which

1

would have prevented any surprise if a long course of inoffensive conduct on his part had ended in the commission of a crime; especially if he had any reputation for knowledge, or showed any skill in handicraft. All cleverness, whether in the rapid use of that difficult instrument the tongue, or in some other art unfamiliar to villagers, was in itself suspicious. Honest folk, born and bred in a visible manner, were mostly not overwise or clever—at least, not beyond such a matter as knowing the signs of the weather. In this way it came to pass that those scattered linen weavers— emigrants from the town into the country—were, to the last, regarded as aliens by their rustic neighbors and usually contracted the eccentric habits that belong to a state of loneliness.

In the early years of this century, such a linen weaver, named Silas Marner, worked at his vocation in a stone cottage that stood among the nutty hedgerows near the village of Raveloe, not far from the edge of a deserted stone pit. The questionable sound of Silas's loom, so unlike the natural cheerful trotting of the winnowing machine, or the simpler rhythm of the flail, had a half-fearful fascination for the Raveloe boys, who would often leave off their nutting or bird's-nesting to peep in at the window of the stone cottage. Sometimes it happened that Marner, pausing to adjust an irregularity in his thread, became aware of the small scoundrels, and, though wary of his time, he liked their intrusion so ill that he would descend from his loom, and, opening the door, would fix on them a gaze that was always enough to make them take to their legs in terror. How was it possible to believe that those large, brown, protuberant eyes in Silas Marner's pale face really saw nothing very distinctly that was not close to them, and not rather that their dreadful stare could dart cramp or rickets or a wry mouth at any boy who happened to be in the rear? They had, perhaps, heard their fathers and mothers hint that Silas Marner could cure folks' rheumatism if he had a mind, and add, still more darkly, that if you could only speak to the devil fair enough, he might save you the cost of the doctor. Such strange lingering echoes of the old demon worship might perhaps even now be caught by the diligent listener among the gray-haired peasantry; for the rude mind with difficulty associates the ideas of power and benignity.

Raveloe was a village where many of the old echoes lingered, undrowned by new voices. Not that it was one of those barren parishes lying on the outskirts of civilization, inhabited by meager sheep and thinly scattered shepherds. On the contrary, it lay in the rich central plain of what we are pleased to call Merry England, and held farms that, speaking from a spiritual point of view, paid highly desirable tithes. It was nestled in a snug, well-wooded hollow, quite an hour's journey on horseback from any turnpike, where it was never reached by the vibrations of the coach horn or of public opinion. It was an important-looking village, with a fine old church and large churchyard in the heart of it, and had two or three large brick-and-stone homesteads, with well-walled orchards and ornamental weathercocks, standing close upon the road, and lifting more imposing fronts than the rectory, which peeped from among the trees on the other side of the churchyard. It was a village that showed at once the summits of its social life and told the practiced eye that there was no great park and manor house in the vicinity, but that there were several chiefs in Raveloe who, though poor farmers, could easily draw enough money from their bad farming to live in a rollicking fashion and keep a jolly Christmas, Whitsun, and Eastertide.

It was fifteen years since Silas Marner had first come to Raveloe. He was then simply a pallid young man with prominent short-sighted brown eyes, whose appearance would have seemed nothing strange for people of average culture and experience, but for the villagers near whom he had come to settle, it had mysterious peculiarities that corresponded with the exceptional nature of his occupation and his advent from an unknown region called "North'ard." So had his way of life. He invited no comer to step across his doorsill, and he never strolled into the village to meet friends at the Rainbow Inn or to gossip at the wheelwright's. He sought no man or woman, save for the purposes of his calling or in order to supply himself with necessaries, and it was soon clear to the Raveloe lasses that he would never urge one of them to accept him against her will—quite as if he had heard them declare that they would never marry a dead man come to life again. This view of Marner's personality was because of his pale face and unexampled eyes; for Jem Rodney, the mole catcher, averred that one evening as he was returning homeward, he saw Silas Marner leaning against a stile with a heavy bag on his back instead of resting the bag on the stile as a man in his senses would have done. On coming up to him, he saw that Marner's eyes were set like a dead man's. He spoke to him and shook him, but his limbs were stiff, and his hands clutched the bag as if they'd been made of iron. Just as he made up his mind that the weaver was dead, he came all right again, like, as you might say, in the winking of an eye, and said "Good night," and walked off. All this Jem swore he had seen the very day he had been mole-catching on Squire Cass's land down by the old saw pit. Some said Marner must have been in a "fit," a word which seemed to explain things otherwise incredible; but the argumentative Mr. Macey, clerk of the parish, shook his head and asked if anybody was ever known to go off in a fit and not fall down. A fit was a stroke, wasn't it? and it was in the nature of a stroke to partly take away the use of a man's limbs and throw him on the parish, if he'd got no children to look to. No, no, it was no stroke that would let a man stand on his legs, like a horse between the shafts, and then walk off as soon as you can say "Gee!" And from where did Master Marner get his knowledge of herbs? Jem Rodney's story was no more than what might have been expected by anybody who had seen how Marner had cured Sally Oates and made her sleep like a baby when her heart had been beating enough to burst her body, for two months and more, while she had been under the doctor's care. He might cure more folks if he would;

and it was best to speak fair of him if it was only to keep him from doing you a mischief.

It was partly to this vague fear that Marner was indebted for protecting him from the persecution that his singularities might have drawn upon him. Still more important was the fact that the old linen weaver in the neighboring parish of Tarley being dead, his handicraft made him a highly welcome settler to the richer housewives of the district, and even to the more provident cottagers, who had their little stock of yarn at the year's end. Their sense of his usefulness would have counteracted any repugnance or suspicion that was not confirmed by a deficiency in the quality or the tale of the cloth he wove for them. The years had rolled on without producing any change in the impressions of the neighbors concerning Marner, except the change from novelty to habit. At the end of fifteen years, the Raveloe men said just the same things about Silas Marner as at the beginning. They did not say them quite so often, but they believed them much more strongly when they did say them. There was only one important addition which the years had brought: it was that Master Marner had laid by a fine sight of money somewhere and that he could buy up "bigger men" than himself.

While opinion concerning him had remained nearly stationary, and his daily habits had presented scarcely any visible change, Marner's inward life had been a history and a metamorphosis, as that of every fervid nature must be when it has fled, or been condemned, to solitude.

Marner, before he came to Raveloe, was highly thought of in that little hidden world known to itself as the church assembling in Lantern Yard. He was believed to be a young man of exemplary life and ardent faith; and a peculiar interest had been centered in him ever since he had fallen, at a prayer meeting, into a mysterious rigidity and suspension of consciousness, which, lasting for an hour or more, had been mistaken for death. To have sought a medical explanation for this phenomenon would have been held by Silas himself, as well as by his minister and fellow members, a willful self-exclusion from the spiritual significance that might lie therein. Silas was evidently a brother selected for a peculiar discipline; and though the effort to interpret this discipline was discouraged by the absence, on his part, of any spiritual vision during his outward trance, yet it was believed by himself and others that its effect was seen in an accession of light and fervor. A less truthful man than he might have been tempted into the subsequent creation of a vision in the form of resurgent memory. A less sane man might have believed in such a creation; but Silas was both sane and honest, though, as with many honest and fervent men, culture had not defined any channels for his sense of mystery, and so it spread itself over the proper pathway of inquiry and knowledge. He had inherited from his mother some acquaintance with medicinal herbs and their preparation—a little store of wisdom which she had imparted to him as a solemn bequest—but of late years he had had doubts about the lawfulness of applying this knowledge, believing that herbs could have no efficacy without prayer and that prayer might suffice without herbs; so that his inherited delight to wander through the fields in search of foxglove and dandelion and coltsfoot began to wear to him the character of a temptation.

Among the members of his church, there was one young man, a little older than himself, with whom he had long lived in such close friendship that it was the custom of their Lantern Yard brethren to call them David and Jonathan. The real name of the friend was

7

William Dane, and he, too, was regarded as a shining instance of youthful piety, though somewhat given to overseverity toward weaker brethren, and to be so dazzled by his own light as to hold himself wiser than his teachers. Whatever blemishes others might discern in William, to his friend's mind he was faultless; for Marner had one of those impressible, self-doubting natures which, at an inexperienced age, admire imperativeness and lean on contradiction. The expression of trusting simplicity in Marner's face, heightened by that absence of special observation, that defenseless, deerlike gaze which belongs to large, prominent eyes, was strongly contrasted by the self-complacent suppression of inward triumph that lurked in the narrow, slanting eyes and compressed lips of William Dane.

It had seemed to the unsuspecting Silas that the friendship had suffered no chill even from his formation of another attachment of a closer kind. For some months he had been engaged to a young servant woman, waiting only for a little increase to their mutual savings in order to set their marriage; and it was a great delight to him that Sarah did not object to William's occasional presence in their Sunday interviews. It was at this point in their history that Silas's cataleptic fit occurred during the prayer meeting; and amidst the various queries and expressions of interest addressed to him by his fellow members, William's suggestion alone jarred general sympathy toward a brother thus singled out for special dealings. He observed that, to him, this trance looked more like a visitation of Satan than a proof of divine favor, and exhorted his friend to see that he hid no accursed thing within his soul. Silas, feeling bound to accept rebuke and admonition as a brotherly office, felt no resentment, but only pain, at his friend's doubts concerning him. To this was soon added some anxiety at the perception that Sarah's manner toward him began to exhibit a strange fluctuation between an effort at an increased manifestation of regard and involuntary signs of shrinking and dislike. He asked her if she wished to break off their engagement, but she denied this. Their engagement was known to the church and had been recognized in the prayer meetings. It could not be broken off without strict investigation, and Sarah could render no reason that would be sanctioned by the feeling of the community.

At this time, the senior deacon was taken dangerously ill, and, being a childless widower, he was tended night and day by some of the younger brethren or sisters. Silas frequently took his turn in the night watching with William, the one relieving the other at two in the morning. The old man, contrary to expectation, seemed to be on the way to recovery when one night, Silas, sitting up by his bedside, observed that his usual audible breathing had ceased. The candle was burning low, and he had to lift it to see the patient's face distinctly. Examination convinced him that the deacon was dead—had been dead some time, for the limbs were rigid. Silas asked himself if he had been asleep and looked at the clock. It was already four in the morning. How was it that William had not come? In much anxiety he went to seek for help, and soon there were several friends assembled in the house, the minister among them, while Silas went away to his work, wishing he could have met William to know the reason of his nonappearance. But at six o'clock, as he was thinking of going to seek his friend, William came, and with him the minister. They came to summon him to Lantern Yard to meet the church members there; and to his inquiry concerning the cause of the summons the only reply was, "You will hear." Nothing further was said until Silas was seated in the vestry, in front of the minister, with the eyes of those who to him represented God's people fixed solemnly upon him. Then the minister, taking out a pocketknife, showed it to Silas and asked him if he knew where he had left that knife? Silas said he did not know that he had left it anywhere out of his own pocket—but he was trembling at this strange interrogation. He was then exhorted not to hide his sin but to confess and repent. The knife had been found in the bureau by the departed deacon's bedside—found in the place where the little bag of church money had lain, which the minister himself had seen the day before. Some hand had removed that bag; and whose hand could it be, if not that of the man to whom the knife belonged? For some time Silas was mute with astonishment; then he said, "God will clear me. I know nothing about the knife being there or the money being gone. Search me and my dwelling; you will find nothing but three pound five of my own savings, which William Dane knows I have had these six months." At this William groaned, but the minister said, "The proof is heavy against you, Brother Marner. The money was taken in the night last past, and no man was with our departed brother but you, for William Dane declares to us that he was hindered by sudden sickness from going to take his place as usual, and you yourself said that he had not come; and, moreover, you neglected the dead body."

"I must have slept," said Silas. Then, after a pause he added, "Or I must have had another visitation like that which you have all seen me under, so that the thief must have come and gone while I was not in the body, but out of the body. I say again, search me and my dwelling, for I have been nowhere else."

The search was made, and it ended—in William Dane's finding the well-known bag, empty, tucked behind the chest of drawers in Silas's chamber! On this

William exhorted his friend to confess and not to hide his sin any longer. Silas turned a look of keen reproach on him and said, "William, for nine years that we have gone in and out together, have you ever known me tell a lie? But God will clear me."

"Brother," said William, "how do I know what you may have done in the secret chambers of your heart, to give Satan an advantage over you?"

Silas was still looking at his friend. Suddenly a deep flush came over his face, and he was about to speak impetuously, when he seemed checked again by some inward shock that sent the flush back and made him tremble. At last he spoke feebly, looking at William.

"I remember now—the knife wasn't in my pocket."

William said, "I know nothing of what you mean." The other persons present, however, began to inquire where Silas meant to say that the knife was, but he would give no further explanation; he only said, "I am sore stricken; I can say nothing. God will clear me."

On their return to the vestry there was further deliberation. Any resort to legal measures for ascertaining the culprit was contrary to the principles of the church in Lantern Yard, according to which prosecution was forbidden to Christians, even had the case held less scandal to the community. The members were bound to take other measures for finding out the truth, and they resolved on praying and drawing lots. This resolution can be a ground of surprise only to those who are unacquainted with religious life that has gone on in our towns. Silas knelt with his brethren, relying on his own innocence being certified by immediate divine interference, but feeling that there was sorrow and mourning ahead for him even then—that his trust in man had been cruelly bruised. *The lots declared that Silas Marner was guilty.* He was solemnly suspended from church membership and called upon to

11

render up the stolen money. Only on confession, as the sign of repentance, could he be received once more within the fold of the church. Marner listened in silence. At last, when everyone rose to depart, he went toward William Dane and said, in a voice shaken by agitation,

"The last time I remember using my knife was when I took it out to cut a strap for you. I don't remember putting it in my pocket again. *You* stole the money, and you have woven a plot to lay the sin at my door."

There was a general shudder at this blasphemy.

William said meekly, "I leave our brethren to judge whether this is the voice of Satan or not. I can do nothing but pray for you, Silas."

Poor Marner went out with that despair in his soul—that shaken trust in God and man that is little short of madness to a loving nature. In the bitterness of his wounded spirit, he said to himself, "*She* will cast me

off too." And he reflected that, if she did not believe the testimony against him, her whole faith must be upset. We are apt to think it inevitable that a man in Marner's position should have begun to question the validity of an appeal to the divine judgment by drawing lots; but to him this would have been an effort of independent thought such as he had never known; and he must have made the effort at a moment when all his energies were turned into anguish. If there is an angel who records the sorrows of men as well as their sins, he knows how many and deep are the sorrows that spring from false ideas for which no man is culpable.

Marner went home, and for a whole day sat alone, stunned by despair, without any impulse to go to Sarah and attempt to win her belief in his innocence. The second day he took refuge from benumbing unbelief by going to his loom and working away as usual. Before many hours were past, the minister and one of the deacons came to him with the message from Sarah that she held her engagement to him at an end. Silas received the message mutely and then turned away from the messengers to work at his loom again. In little more than a month from that time, Sarah was married to William Dane; and not long afterward it was known to the brethren in Lantern Yard that Silas Marner had departed from the town.

Chapter 2

Even people whose lives have been made various by learning sometimes find it hard to keep a fast hold on their habitual views of life and on their faith in the Invisible. They lose the sense that their past joys and sorrows are a real experience when they are suddenly transported to a new land where the beings around them know nothing of their history and share none of their ideas—where their mother earth shows another lap, and human life has other forms than those on which their souls have been nourished. Minds that have been unhinged from their old faith and love have perhaps sought exile, and the past becomes dreamy because its symbols have all vanished, and the present, too, is dreamy because it is linked with no memories. Still, those who have experienced this can hardly imagine what was the effect on a simple weaver like Silas Marner when he left his own country and people and came to settle in Raveloe.

Nothing could be more unlike his native town, which was set within sight of the widespread hillsides. In this low, wooded region, he felt hidden even from the heavens by the screening trees and hedgerows. There was nothing here. When he rose in the deep morning quiet and looked out on the dewy brambles and rank, all he saw was tufted grass that didn't seem to have any relation with that life centering in Lantern Yard—which had once been to him the altar place of high dispensations. The whitewashed walls; the little pews where well-known figures entered with a subdued rustling and where first one well-known voice and then another, pitched in a peculiar key of petition, uttered phrases familiar, like the amulet worn on the heart; the pulpit where the minister delivered unquestioned doctrine and swayed to and fro and handled the book in a long-accustomed manner; the very pauses between the couplets of the hymn as it was given out and the recurrent swell of voices in song. These things had been the channel of divine influences to Marner. They were the fostering home of his religious emotions. They were Christianity and God's kingdom upon earth.

And what could be more unlike that Lantern Yard world than the world in Raveloe? Here were orchards looking lazy with neglected plenty; the large church in the wide churchyard, which men gazed at, lounging at their own doors in service time; the purple-faced farmers jogging along the lanes or turning in at the Rainbow; homesteads, where men supped heavily and slept in the light of the evening hearth, and where women seemed to be laying up a stock of linen for the life to come. There were no lips in Raveloe from which a word could fall that could stir Silas Marner's benumbed faith from his pain. It seemed to him that the Power he had vainly trusted in among the streets and at the prayer meetings in Lantern Yard was very far away from this land in which he had taken refuge. Here men lived in careless abundance, knowing and needing nothing of that trust, which, for him, had been turned to bitterness. The little light he possessed spread its beams so narrowly that frustrated belief was a curtain broad enough to create for him the blackness of night.

His first movement after the shock had been to work at his loom, and he went on with this unremittingly, never asking himself why. Now that he was come to Raveloe, he worked far on into the night to finish the tale of Mrs. Osgood's table linen sooner than she expected—without contemplating beforehand the money she would put into his hand for the work. He seemed to weave, like the spider, from pure impulse, without reflection. Every man's work, pursued steadily, tends in this way to become an end in itself, and so to bridge over the loveless chasms of his life. Silas's hand satisfied itself with throwing the shuttle, and his eye was gratified with seeing the little squares in the cloth complete themselves under his effort. Then there were the calls of hunger. Silas, in his solitude, had to provide his own breakfast, dinner, and supper; to fetch his own water from the well; and to put his own kettle on the fire. All these immediate promptings helped, along with the weaving, to reduce his life to the unquestioning activity of a spinning insect. He hated the thoughts of the past. There was nothing that called out his love and fellowship toward the strangers he had come among, and the future was all dark, for there was no Unseen Love that cared for him. Thought was arrested by utter bewilderment, now its old, narrow pathway was closed; and affection seemed to have died under the bruise that had fallen on its keenest nerves.

At last Mrs. Osgood's table linen was finished, and Silas was paid in gold. His earnings in his native town, where he worked for a wholesale dealer, had been after a lower rate; he had been paid weekly, and of his weekly earnings a large proportion had gone to objects of piety and charity. Now, for the first time in his life, he had five bright guineas put into his hand; no man expected a share of them, and he loved no man that he should offer him a share. But what were the guineas to him who saw no vista beyond countless days of weaving? It was needless for him to ask that, for it was pleasant to him to feel them in his palm and to look at their bright faces, which were all his own. It was another element of life, like the weaving and the satisfaction of hunger, subsisting quite aloof from the life of belief and love from which he had been cut off. The weaver's hand had known the touch of hard-won money even before the palm had grown to its full breadth. For twenty years money had stood to him as the symbol of earthly good and the immediate object of toil. He had seemed to love it little in the years when every penny had its purpose for him, for he loved the *purpose* then. But now, when all purpose was gone, that habit of looking toward the money and grasping it with a sense of fulfilled effort made a loam that was deep enough for the seeds of desire; and as Silas walked homeward across the fields in the twilight, he drew out the money and thought it was brighter in the gathering gloom.

About this time an incident happened which seemed to open a possibility of some fellowship with his neighbors. One day, taking a pair of shoes to be

17

mended, he saw the cobbler's wife seated by the fire, suffering from the terrible symptoms of heart disease and dropsy, which he had witnessed as the precursors of his mother's death. He felt a rush of pity at the mingled sight and remembrance, and, recalling the relief his mother had found from a simple preparation of foxglove, he promised Sally Oates to bring her something that would ease her, since the doctor did her no good. In this office of charity, Silas felt, for the first time since he had come to Raveloe, a sense of unity between his past and present life, which might have been the beginning of his rescue from the insectlike existence into which his nature had shrunk. Sally Oates's disease had raised her into a personage of much interest and importance among the neighbors, and the fact of her having found relief from drinking Silas Marner's "stuff" became a matter of general discourse. When Doctor Kimble gave physic, it was natural that it should have an effect; but when a weaver, who came from nobody knew where, worked wonders with a bottle of brown waters, the occult character of the process seemed evident. Such a sort of thing had not been known since the Wise Woman at Tarley died; and she had "charms" as well as "stuff"; everybody went to her when their children had "fits." Silas Marner must be a person of the same sort, for how did he know what would bring back Sally Oates's breath, if he didn't know a fine sight more than that? The Wise Woman had words that she muttered to herself, so that you couldn't hear what they were; and if she tied a bit of red thread round the child's toe for a while, it would keep off the water in the head. There were women in Raveloe, at that present time, who had worn one of the Wise Woman's little bags around their necks, and, in consequence, had never had an idiot child, as Ann Coulter had. Silas Marner could very likely do as much, and more. Now it was all clear how he should have come from unknown parts and be so "comical-looking." Sally Oates must mind and not tell the doctor, for he would be sure to set his face against Marner; he was always angry about the Wise Woman, and used to threaten those who went to her that they should have none of his help anymore.

Silas now found himself and his cottage suddenly beset by mothers who wanted him to charm away the whooping cough, and by men who wanted stuff against the rheumatics or the knots in the hands; and, to secure themselves against a refusal, the applicants brought silver in their palms. Silas might have driven a profitable trade in charms as well as in his small list of drugs; but money on this condition was no temptation to him. He had never known an impulse toward falsity, and he drove one after another away with growing irritation, for the news of him as a wise man had spread even to Tarley, and it was long before people ceased to take long walks for the sake of asking his aid. The hope in his wisdom was at length changed into dread, for no one believed him when he said he knew no charms and could work no cures, and every man and woman who had an accident or a new attack after going to him, set the misfortune down to Master Marner's ill will and irritated glances. Thus, it came to pass that his movement of pity toward Sally Oates, which had given him a transient sense of brotherhood, heightened the repulsion between him and his neighbors and made his isolation more complete.

Gradually the guineas, the crowns, and the half crowns grew to a heap; and Marner drew less and less for his own wants, trying to solve the problem of keeping himself strong enough to work sixteen hours a day on as small an outlay as possible. Have not men, shut up in solitary imprisonment, found an interest in marking the moments by straight strokes of a certain length on the wall until the growth of the sum of straight strokes, arranged in triangles, has become a mastering purpose? Do we not while away moments of inanity or fatigued waiting by repeating some trivial movement or sound until the repetition has bred a want which is incipient habit? That will help us to understand how the love of accumulation of money grows into an absorbing passion in men whose imaginations, even in the very beginning of their hoard, showed them no purpose beyond it. Marner wanted the heaps of ten to grow into a square, and then into a larger square; and every added guinea, while it was itself a satisfaction, bred a new desire. In this strange world—made a hopeless riddle to him—he might, if he had had a less intense nature, have sat weaving, weaving—looking toward the end of his pattern, or toward the end of his web, till he forgot the riddle and everything else but his immediate sensations. But the money had come to mark off his weaving into periods, and the money not only grew, but it remained with him. He began to think it was conscious of him, as his loom was, and he would on no account have exchanged those coins, which had become his familiars, for other coins with unknown faces. He handled them, he counted them till their form and color were like the satisfaction of a thirst to him; but it was only in the night, when his work was done, that he drew them out to enjoy their companionship. He had taken up some bricks in his floor underneath his loom, and here he had made a hole in which he set the iron pot that contained his guineas and silver coins, covering the bricks with sand whenever he replaced them. Not that the idea of being robbed presented itself often or strongly to his mind; hoarding was common in country districts in those days. There were old laborers in the parish of Raveloe who were known to have their savings by them, probably inside their flock beds; but their rustic neighbors, though not all of them as honest as their ancestors in the days of King Alfred, had not imaginations bold enough to lay a plan of burglary. How could they have spent the money in their own village without betraying themselves? They would be obliged to "run away"—a course as dark and dubious as a balloon journey.

So year after year, Silas Marner had lived in this solitude, his guineas rising in the iron pot, and his life narrowing and hardening itself more and more into a mere pulsation of desire and into satisfaction that had no relation to any other being. His life had reduced itself to the mere functions of weaving and hoarding, without any contemplation of an end toward which the functions tended. The same sort of process has perhaps been undergone by wiser men when they have been cut off from faith and love—only, instead of a loom and a heap of guineas, they have had some erudite research, some ingenious project, or some well-knit theory. Strangely, Marner's face and figure shrank and bent themselves into a constant mechanical relation to the objects of his life so that he produced the same sort of impression as a handle or a crooked tube, that has no meaning by itself. His prominent eyes that used to look trusting and dreamy now looked as if they had been made to see only one kind of thing—something that was very small, like tiny grain, for which they hunted everywhere; and he was so withered and yellow that, though he was not yet forty, the children always called him "Old Master Marner."

Yet even in this stage of withering, a little incident happened that showed the sap of affection was not all gone. It was one of his daily tasks to fetch his water from a well a couple of fields off, and for this purpose, ever since he came to Raveloe, he had a brown earthenware pot that he held as his most precious utensil among the very few conveniences he had granted himself. It had been his companion for twelve years, always standing on the same spot, always lending its handle to him in the early morning. Its form had an expression for him of willing helpfulness, and the impress of its handle on his palm gave a satisfaction mingled with that of having the fresh, clear water. One day as he was returning from the well, he stumbled against the step of the stile, and his brown pot, falling with force against the stones that overarched the ditch below him, was broken in three pieces. Silas picked up the pieces and carried them home with grief in his heart. The brown pot could never be of use to him any more, but he stuck the bits together and propped the ruin in its old place for a memorial.

This is the history of Silas Marner until the fifteenth year after his coming to Raveloe. The livelong day he sat at his loom, his ear filled with its monotony, his eyes bent close down on the slow growth of sameness in the brownish web, his muscles moving with such even repetition that their pause seemed almost as much a constraint as the holding of his breath. At night came his revelry. At night he closed his shutters and made fast his doors and drew forth his gold. Long ago the heap of coins had become too large for the iron pot to hold them, and he had made for them two thick leather bags, which wasted no room in their resting place, but lent themselves flexibly to every corner. How the guineas shone as they came pouring out of the dark leather mouths! The silver bore no large proportion in amount to the gold, because the long pieces of linen that formed his chief work were always partly paid for in gold. Out of the silver he supplied his own bodily wants, choosing always the shillings and sixpences to spend in this way. He loved the guineas best, but he would not change the silver—the crowns and half crowns that were his own earnings, begotten by his labor; he loved them all. He spread them out in heaps and bathed his hands in them; then he counted them and set them up in regular piles, and felt their rounded outline between his thumb and fingers. He thought fondly of the guineas that were only half-earned by the work at his loom, as if they had been unborn children—thought of the guineas that were coming slowly through the coming years, through all his life, which spread far away before him, the end quite hidden by countless days of weaving. No wonder his thoughts were still with his loom and his money when he made his journeys through the fields and the lanes to fetch and carry home his work. His steps never wandered to the hedge banks and the laneside in search of the once familiar herbs; these, too, belonged to the past from which his life had shrunk away.

About the Christmas of that fifteenth year, a second great change came over Marner's life, and his history became blended in a singular manner with the life of his neighbors.

Chapter 3

The greatest man in Raveloe was Squire Cass, who lived in the large red house with the handsome flight of stone steps in front and the high stables behind it, nearly opposite the church. He was only one among several landed parishioners, but he alone was honored with the title of Squire; for though Mr. Osgood's family was also understood to be of timeless origin—the Raveloe imagination having never ventured back to that fearful blank when there were no Osgoods—he merely owned the farm he occupied; whereas Squire Cass had a tenant or two, who complained of the game to him quite as if he had been a lord.

Raveloe lay low among the bushy trees and the rutted lanes, aloof from the currents of industrial energy and Puritan earnestness. The rich ate and drank freely, accepting gout and apoplexy as things that ran mysteriously in respectable families, and the poor thought that the rich were entirely in the right of it to lead a jolly life; besides, their feasting caused a multiplication of benefits, which were the heirlooms of the poor. Betty Jay scented the boiling of Squire Cass's hams, but her longing was arrested by the unctuous liquid in which they were boiled; and when the seasons brought round the great merrymakings, they were regarded on all hands as a fine thing for the poor. For the Raveloe feasts were on a large scale and lasted a good while, especially in the wintertime. After ladies had packed up their best gowns and topknots in bandboxes and had incurred the risk of fording streams on pillions with the precious burden in rainy or snowy weather, when there was no knowing how high the water would rise, it was accepted that they looked forward to a brief pleasure. On this ground, it was always contrived in the dark seasons—when there was

25

little work to be done and the hours were long—that several neighbors should keep open house in succession. So soon as Squire Cass's standing dishes diminished in plenty and freshness, his guests had nothing to do but to walk a little higher up the village to Mr. Osgood's at The Orchards. There they found hams and chines uncut, pork pies with the scent of the fire in them, spun butter in all its freshness—everything, in fact, that appetites at leisure could desire, in perhaps greater perfection, though not in greater abundance, than at Squire Cass's.

The Squire's wife had died long ago, and Red House was without that presence of the wife and mother that is the fountain of wholesome love and fear in parlor and kitchen. This helped to account not only for there being more profusion than finished excellence in the holiday provisions, but also for the frequency with which the proud Squire condescended to preside in the parlor of the Rainbow rather than under the shadow of his own dark wainscot; perhaps, also, for the fact that his sons had turned out rather ill. Raveloe was not a place where moral censure was severe, but it was thought a weakness in the Squire that he had kept all his sons at home in idleness; and though some license was to be allowed to young men whose fathers could afford it, people shook their heads at the course of the second son, Dunstan, commonly called Dunsey Cass, whose taste for swapping and betting might turn out to be a sowing of something worse than wild oats. To be sure, the neighbors said it was no matter what became of Dunsey—a spiteful, jeering fellow who seemed to enjoy his drink the more when other people went dry—provided that his doings did not bring trouble on a family like Squire Cass's, with a monument in the church and tankards older than King George. It would be a thousand pities if Mr. Godfrey, the eldest, a fine, open-faced, good-natured young man, who was to come into the land some day, should take to going along the same road with his brother, as he had seemed to do of late. If he went on in that way, he would lose Miss Nancy Lammeter; for it was well known that she had looked very shyly on him ever since last Whitsuntide twelvemonth, when there was so much talk about his being away from home days and days together. There was something wrong—that was quite clear; for Mr. Godfrey didn't look half so fresh-colored and open as he used to do. At one time, everybody was saying what a handsome couple he and Miss Nancy Lammeter would make, and if she could come to be mistress at Red House there would be a fine change, for the Lammeters had been brought up in that way that they never suffered a pinch of salt to be wasted, and yet everybody in their household had of the best, according to his place. Such a daughter-in-law would be a saving to the old Squire even if she never brought a penny to her fortune; for it was to be feared that, notwithstanding his incomings, there were more holes in his pocket than the one where he put his own hand in. But if Mr. Godfrey didn't turn over a new leaf, he might say "Good-by" to Miss Nancy Lammeter.

It was the once-hopeful Godfrey who was standing—with his hands in his side pockets and his back to the fire—in the dark wainscoted parlor, one late November afternoon in that fifteenth year of Silas Marner's life at Raveloe. The fading gray light fell dimly on the walls decorated with guns, whips, and foxes' brushes, on coats and hats flung on the chairs, and on a half-choked fire: signs of a domestic life destitute of any hallowing charm, with which the look of gloomy vexation on Godfrey's blond face was in sad accordance. He seemed to be waiting and listening for someone's approach, and presently the sound of a heavy step, with an

27

accompanying whistle, was heard across the large, empty entrance hall.

The door opened, and a thick-set, heavy-looking young man entered, with the flushed face and the gratuitously elated bearing which marked the first stage of intoxication. It was Dunsey, and at the sight of him Godfrey's face parted with some of its gloom to take on the more active expression of hatred. The handsome brown spaniel that lay on the hearth retreated under the chair in the chimney corner.

"Well, Master Godfrey, what do you want with me?" said Dunsey in a mocking tone. "You're my elder and better, you know; I was obligated to come when you sent for me."

"This is what I want. Shake yourself sober and listen, will you?" said Godfrey savagely. He had himself been drinking more than was good for him, trying to turn his gloom into uncalculating anger. "I want to tell you that I must hand over that rent of Fowler's to the Squire or else tell him I gave it you; for he's threatening to distrain for it, and it'll all be out soon, whether I tell him or not. He said, just now, before he went out, he should send word to Cox to distrain, if Fowler didn't come and pay up his arrears this week. The Squire's short o' cash and in no humor to stand any nonsense; and you know what he threatened if ever he found you making away with his money again. So, get the money, and pretty quickly, will you?"

"Oh!" said Dunsey sneeringly, coming nearer to his brother and looking in his face. "Suppose, now, you get the money yourself and save me the trouble, eh? Since you were so kind as to hand it over to me, you'll not refuse me the kindness to pay it back for me. It was your brotherly love made you do it, you know."

Godfrey bit his lips and clenched his fist. "Don't come near me with that look, else I'll knock you down."

"Oh, no, you won't," said Dunsey, turning away on his heel. "Because I'm such a good-natured brother, you know I might get you turned out of house and home and cut off with a shilling any day. I might tell the Squire how his handsome son was 'happily' married to that 'nice young' Molly Farren—a woman who was too drunk to live with. Then I should slip into your place as comfortable as could be. But you see, I won't do it—I'm so easy and good-natured. You'll take any trouble for me. You'll get the hundred pounds for me—I know you will."

"How can I get the money?" said Godfrey, quivering. "I haven't a shilling. It's a lie that you'd slip into my place; you'd get yourself turned out too, that's all. For if you begin telling tales, I'll follow. Bob's my father's favorite—you know that very well. He'd only think himself well rid of you."

"Never mind," said Dunsey, nodding his head sideways as he looked out of the window. "It'ud be very pleasant to me to go in your company—you're such a handsome brother, and we've always been so fond of quarreling with one another. I shouldn't know what to do without you. You'd like better for us both to stay at home together; I know you would. So you'll manage to get that little sum o' money, and I'll bid you good-by, though I'm sorry to part."

Dunstan was moving off, but Godfrey rushed after him and seized him by the arm, saying,—

"I tell you, I have no money; I can get no money."

"Borrow of old Kimble."

"I tell you, he won't lend me any more, and I shan't ask him."

"Well, then, sell Wildfire."

"Yes, that's easy talking. I must have the money directly."

"Well, you've only got to ride him to the hunt tomorrow. There'll be Bryce and Keating there, for sure. You'll get more bids than one."

"I daresay, and get back home at eight o'clock, splashed up to the chin. I'm going to Mrs. Osgood's birthday party."

"Oho!" said Dunsey, turning his head on one side and trying to speak in a small mincing treble. "And there's sweet Miss Nancy coming; and we shall smile at her, and promise never to be naughty again, and be taken into favor, and—"

"Hold your tongue about Miss Nancy, you fool," said Godfrey, turning red, "else I'll throttle you."

"What for?" said Dunsey, still in an artificial tone, but taking a whip from the table and beating the butt end of it on his palm. "You've a very good chance. I'd advise you to creep up her sleeve again. It 'ud be saving time if Molly should happen to take a drop too much laudanum some day and make a widower of you. Miss Nancy wouldn't mind being a second, if she didn't know it, and you've got a good-natured brother, who'll keep your secret well, because you'll be so very obliging to him."

"I'll tell you what it is," said Godfrey, quivering and pale again, "my patience is pretty near at an end. If you'd a little more sharpness in you, you might know that you may urge a man a bit too far and make one leap as easy as another. I don't know but what it is so now; I may as well tell the Squire everything myself. I should get you off my back, if I got nothing else. And, after all, he'll know some time. She's been threatening to come herself and tell him. So don't flatter yourself that your secrecy's worth any price you choose to ask. You drain me of money till I have got nothing to pacify *her* with, and she'll do as she threatens some day. It's all one. I'll tell my father everything myself."

Dunsey perceived that he had overshot his mark and that there was a point at which even the hesitating Godfrey might be driven into decision. He said, with an air of unconcern:

"As you please." And ringing the bell, he threw himself across two chairs and began to rap the window seat with the handle of his whip.

Godfrey stood, still with his back to the fire, uneasily moving his fingers among the contents of his side pockets and looking at the floor. That big muscular frame of his held plenty of animal courage, but helped him to no decision when the dangers to be braved were such as could neither be knocked down nor throttled. His natural irresolution and moral cowardice were exaggerated by a position in which dreaded consequences seemed to press equally on all sides, and his irritation had no sooner provoked him to defy Dunstan and anticipate all possible betrayals than the miseries he must bring on himself by such a step seemed more unendurable to him than the present evil. The results of confession were not contingent, they were certain; whereas betrayal was not certain. From the near vision of that certainty he fell back on suspense and vacillation with a sense of repose.

The disinherited son of a small squire, equally disinclined to dig and to beg, was almost as helpless as an uprooted tree, which, by the favor of the earth and sky, has grown to a handsome bulk on the spot where it first shot upward. Perhaps it would have been possible to think of digging with some cheerfulness if Nancy Lammeter were to be won on those terms; but, since he must irrevocably lose *her*, as well as the inheritance, and must break every tie but the one that degraded him and left him without motive for trying to recover his better self, he could imagine no future for himself on the other side of confession but that of

31

"'listing for a soldier"—the most desperate step in the eyes of respectable families. No! he would rather trust to casualties than to his own resolve—rather go on sitting at the feast, though with the sword hanging over him and terror in his heart, than rush away into the cold darkness where there was no pleasure left. The utmost concession to Dunstan about the horse began to seem easy compared with the fulfillment of his own threat. But his pride would not let him recommence the conversation otherwise than by continuing the quarrel. Dunstan was waiting for this.

"It's just like you," Godfrey burst out, in a bitter tone, "to talk about my selling Wildfire in that cool way—the last thing I've got to call my own and the best bit of horseflesh I ever had in my life. If you'd got a spark of pride in you, you'd be ashamed to see the stables emptied and everybody sneering about it. It's my belief you'd sell yourself, if it was only for the pleasure of making somebody feel he'd got a bad bargain."

"Ay, ay," said Dunstan, very placably, "you do me justice, I see. You know I'm a jewel for 'ticing people into bargains. For which reason I advise you to let *me* sell Wildfire. I'd ride him to the hunt tomorrow for you, with pleasure. I shouldn't look so handsome as you in the saddle, but it's the horse they'll bid for and not the rider."

"Yes, I dare say—trust my horse to you!"

"As you please," said Dunstan, rapping the window seat again with an air of great unconcern. "It's *you* have got to pay Fowler's money; it's none of my business. You received the money from him when you went to Bramcote, and *you* told the Squire it wasn't paid. I'd nothing to do with that; you chose to be so obliging as to give it to me, that was all. If you don't want to pay the money, let it alone; it's all one to me.

I'm willing to accommodate you by undertaking to sell the horse, seeing it's not convenient for you to go so far tomorrow."

Godfrey was silent for some moments. He would have liked to spring on Dunstan, wrench the whip from his hand, and flog him to within an inch of his life. No bodily fear could have deterred him, but he was mastered by another sort of fear, which was fed by feelings stronger even than his resentment. When he spoke again it was in a half-conciliatory tone.

"Well, you mean no nonsense about the horse, eh? You'll sell him all fair and hand over the money? If you don't, you know, everything 'ull go to smash, for I've got nothing else to trust to; and you'll have less pleasure in pulling the house over my head when your own skull's to be broken too."

"Ay, ay," said Dunstan rising. "All right. I thought you'd come around. I'm the fellow to bring old Bryce up to the scratch. I'll get you a hundred and twenty for him, if I get you a penny."

"But it'll perhaps rain cats and dogs tomorrow, as it did yesterday, and then you can't go," said Godfrey, hardly knowing whether he wished for that obstacle or not.

"Not *it*," said Dunstan. "I'm always lucky in my weather. It might rain if you wanted to go yourself. You've got the beauty, you see, and I've got the luck, so you must keep me by you for your crooked sixpence; you'll *nev*-er get along without me."

"Confound you, hold your tongue!" said Godfrey impetuously. "And take care to keep sober tomorrow, else you'll get pitched on your head coming home, and Wildfire might be the worse for it."

"Make your tender heart easy," said Dunstan, opening the door. "You never knew me see double when I'd got a bargain to make; it 'ud spoil the fun. Besides, whenever I fall, I'm warranted to fall on my legs."

With that, Dunstan slammed the door behind him and left Godfrey to that bitter rumination on his personal circumstances, which was now unbroken from day to day save by the excitement of seeing Miss Nancy Lammeter.

That was the condition of Godfrey Cass in this six and twentieth year of his life. A movement of compunction, helped by those small indefinable influences, which every personal relation exerts on a pliant nature, had urged him into a secret marriage that was a blight on his life. It was an ugly story of low passion, delusion, and waking from delusion, which needs not to be dragged from the privacy of Godfrey's bitter memory. He had long known that the delusion was partly due to a trap laid for him by Dunstan, who saw in his brother's degrading marriage the means of gratifying at once his jealous hate and his cupidity. If Godfrey could have felt himself simply a victim, the iron bit that destiny had put into his mouth would have chafed him less intolerably. If the angry words he muttered half aloud when he was alone had had no other object than Dunstan's diabolical cunning, he might have shrunk less from the consequences of avowal. But he had something else at which to be angry—his own vicious folly, which now seemed as mad and unaccountable to him as almost all our follies and vices do when their promptings have long passed away. For four years he had thought of Nancy Lammeter and wooed her with tacit, patient worship as the woman who made him think of the future with joy. She would be his wife and would make home lovely to him, as his father's home had never been; and it would be easy, when she was always near, to shake off those foolish habits that were no pleasures, but only a feverish way of annulling vacancy. Godfrey's was an essentially domestic nature, bred up in a home where the hearth had no smiles and where the daily habits were not chastised by the presence of household order. His easy disposition made him fall in unresistingly with the family courses, but the need of some tender, permanent affection, the longing for some influence that would make the good he preferred easy to pursue, caused the neatness, purity, and liberal orderliness of the Lammeter household—sunned by the smile of Nancy—to seem like those fresh bright hours of the morning when temptations go to sleep and leave the ear open to the voice of the good angel, inviting to industry, sobriety, and peace. Yet the hope of this paradise had not been enough to save him from a course that shut him out of it forever. Instead of keeping fast hold of the strong silken rope by which Nancy would have drawn him safe

to the green banks—where it was easy to step firmly—
he had let himself be dragged back into mud and slime
in which it was useless to struggle. He had made ties
for himself that robbed him of all wholesome motive
and were a constant exasperation.

Still, there was one position worse than the present: it
was the position he would be in when the ugly secret
was disclosed; and the desire that continually triumphed
over every other was that of warding off the evil day
when he would have to bear the consequences of his
father's violent resentment for the wound inflicted on
his family pride. He would, perhaps, have to turn his
back on that hereditary ease and dignity which, after
all, was a sort of reason for living and would carry
with him the certainty that he was banished forever
from the sight and esteem of Nancy Lammeter. The
longer the interval, the more chance there was of
deliverance from some, at least, of the hateful
consequences to which he had sold himself; the more
opportunities remained for him to snatch the strange
gratification of seeing Nancy and gathering some faint
indications of her lingering regard. Toward this
gratification he was impelled fitfully, every now and
then, after having passed weeks in which he had
avoided her as the far-off, bright-winged prize that only
made him spring forward and find his chain all the
more galling. One of those fits of yearning was on him
now, and it would have been strong enough to have
persuaded him to trust Wildfire to Dunstan rather than
disappoint the yearning, even if he had not had another
reason for his disinclination toward the morrow's hunt.
That other reason was the fact that the morning's meet
was near Batherley, the market town where the unhappy
woman lived—the woman whose image became more
odious to him every day. To his thought the whole
vicinage was haunted by her. The yoke a man creates

36

for himself by wrongdoing will breed hate in the kindliest nature; and the good-humored, affectionate-hearted Godfrey Cass was fast becoming a bitter man, visited by cruel wishes that seemed to enter and depart and enter again like demons who had found in him a ready-garnished home.

What was he to do this evening to pass the time? He might as well go to the Rainbow and hear the talk about the cockfighting. Everybody was there, and what else was there to be done? Though, for his own part, he did not care a button for cockfighting. Snuff, the brown spaniel, who had placed herself in front of him and had been watching him for some time, now jumped up in impatience for the expected caress; but Godfrey thrust her away without looking at her and left the room, followed humbly by the unresenting Snuff, perhaps because she saw no other career open to her.

Chapter 4

Dunstan Cass, setting off in the raw morning, at the judiciously quiet pace of a man who is obliged to ride to cover on his hunter, had to take his way along the lane that, at its farther extremity, passed by the piece of unenclosed ground called the stone pit, where stood the cottage—once a stonecutter's shed—now for fifteen years inhabited by Silas Marner. The spot looked very dreary at this season, with the moist, trodden clay about it, and the red, muddy water high up in the deserted quarry. That was Dunstan's first thought as he approached it; the second was that the old fool of a weaver, whose loom he heard rattling already, had a great deal of money hidden somewhere. How was it that he, Dunstan Cass, who had often heard talk of Marner's miserliness, had never thought of suggesting to Godfrey that he should frighten or persuade the old fellow into lending the money on the excellent security of the young Squire's prospects? The resource occurred to him now as so easy and agreeable—especially as Marner's hoard was likely to be large enough to leave Godfrey a handsome surplus beyond his immediate needs and enable him to accommodate his faithful brother—that he had almost turned the horse's head toward home again. Godfrey would be ready enough to accept the suggestion; he would snatch eagerly at a plan that might save him from parting with Wildfire. But when Dunstan's meditation reached this point, the inclination to go on grew strong and prevailed. He didn't want to give Godfrey that pleasure: he preferred that Master Godfrey should be vexed. Moreover, Dunstan enjoyed the self-important consciousness of having a horse to sell and the opportunity of driving a bargain, swaggering, and possibly taking somebody in. He might have all the satisfaction attendant on selling his brother's horse and not the less have the further satisfaction of getting Godfrey to borrow Marner's money. So he rode on to cover.

Bryce and Keating were there, as Dunstan was quite sure they would be. He felt he was such a "lucky" fellow.

"Heyday!" said Bryce, who had long had his eye on Wildfire, "You're on your brother's horse today. How's that?"

"Oh, I've swapped with him," said Dunstan, whose delight in lying, grandly independent of utility, was not to be diminished by the likelihood that his hearer would not believe him. "Wildfire's mine now."

"What! Has he swapped with you for that big-boned hack of yours?" said Bryce, quite aware that he should get another lie in answer.

"Oh, there was a little account between us," said Dunsey carelessly, "and Wildfire made it even. I accommodated him by taking the horse, though it was against my will, for I'd got an itch for a mare o' Jortin's—as rare a bit o' blood as ever you threw your leg across. But I shall keep Wildfire, now I've got him, though I'd a bid of a hundred and fifty for him the other day, from a man over at Flitton. He's buying for Lord Cromleck—a fellow with a cast in his eye and a green waistcoat. I mean to stick to Wildfire; I shan't get a better at a fence in a hurry. The mare's got more blood, but she's a bit too weak in the hindquarters."

Bryce, of course, divined that Dunstan wanted to sell the horse, and Dunstan knew that he divined it (horse dealing is only one of many human transactions carried on in this ingenious manner); and they both considered that the bargain was in its first stage when Bryce replied ironically:

"I wonder at that now; I wonder you mean to keep him, for I never heard of a man who didn't want to sell his horse getting a bid of half as much again as the horse was worth. You'll be lucky if you get a hundred."

Keating rode up now, and the transaction became more complicated. It ended in the purchase of the horse by Bryce for a hundred and twenty, to be paid on delivery of Wildfire, safe and sound, at the Batherley stables. It did occur to Dunsey that it might be wise for him to give up the day's hunting, proceed at once to Batherley, and, having waited for Bryce's return, hire a horse to carry him home with the money in his pocket. But the inclination for a run, encouraged by the false confidence in his luck, brought on by a draught of brandy from his pocket pistol at the conclusion of the bargain, was not easy to overcome, especially with a horse under him that would take the fences to the

40

admiration of the field. Dunstan, however, took one fence too many and got his horse pierced with a hedge stake. His own ill-favored person, which was quite unmarketable, escaped without injury; but poor Wildfire, unconscious of his price, turned on his flank and painfully panted his last.

It happened that Dunstan, a short time before, having had to get down to arrange his stirrup, had muttered angrily at this interruption, which had thrown him in the rear of the hunt near the moment of glory. Under this exasperation he had taken the fences more blindly. He would soon have been up with the hounds again, when the fatal accident happened. Hence, he was between eager riders in advance, who did not trouble themselves about what happened behind them, and far-off stragglers, who were as likely as not to pass quite aloof from the line of road in which Wildfire had fallen. Dunstan, whose nature it was to care more for immediate annoyances than for remote consequences, no sooner recovered his legs, and saw that it was all over with Wildfire, than he felt a satisfaction at the absence of witnesses to a position which no swaggering could make enviable. Reinforcing himself, after his shake, with a little brandy, he walked as fast as he could to a coppice on his right hand, through which it occurred to him that he could make his way to Batherley without danger of encountering any member of the hunt. His first intention was to hire a horse there and ride home forthwith, for to walk many miles without a gun in his hand and along an ordinary road was as much out of the question to him as to other spirited young men of his kind. He did not much mind about taking the bad news to Godfrey, for he had to offer him at the same time the resource of Marner's money. If Godfrey kicked, as he always did at the notion of making a fresh debt from which he himself got the smallest share of advantage, why, he wouldn't kick long. Dunstan felt sure he could worry Godfrey into anything. The idea of Marner's money kept growing in vividness, now the want of it had become immediate. The prospect of having to make his appearance with the muddy boots of a pedestrian at Batherley and to encounter the grinning queries of stablemen, stood unpleasantly in the way of his impatience to be back at Raveloe and carry out his felicitous plan; and a casual visitation of his waistcoat pocket, as he was ruminating, awakened his memory to the fact that the two or three small coins his forefinger encountered there were of too pale a color to cover that small debt, without payment of which the stablekeeper had declared he would never do any more business with Dunsey Cass. After all, according to the direction in which the run had brought him, he was not so very much farther from home than he was from Batherley; but Dunsey, not being remarkable for clearness of head, was only led to this conclusion by the gradual perception that there were other reasons for choosing the unprecedented course of walking home.

It was now nearly four o'clock, and a mist was gathering; the sooner he got into the road the better. He remembered having crossed the road and seen the finger post only a little while before Wildfire broke down; so, buttoning his coat, twisting the lash of his hunting whip compactly round the handle, and rapping the tops of his boots with a self-possessed air, as if to assure himself that he was not at all taken by surprise, he set off with the sense that he was undertaking a remarkable feat of bodily exertion. Somehow and at some time he should be able to dress up and magnify to the admiration of a select circle at the Rainbow. When a young gentleman like Dunsey is reduced to so exceptional a mode of locomotion as walking, a whip in his hand is a desirable corrective to a too bewildering dreamy sense

42

of unwontedness; and Dunstan, as he went along through the gathering mist, was always rapping his whip somewhere. It was Godfrey's whip, which he had chosen to take without leave because it had a gold handle. Of course no one could see, when Dunstan held it, that the name *Godfrey Cass* was cut in deep letters on that gold handle—they could only see that it was a very handsome whip. Dunsey was not without fear that he might meet some acquaintance in whose eyes he would cut a pitiable figure, for mist is no screen when people get close to each other; but when he at last found himself in the well-known Raveloe lanes without having met a soul, he silently remarked that that was part of his usual good luck. But now the mist, helped by the evening darkness, was more of a screen than he desired, for it hid the ruts into which his feet were liable to slip—hid everything, so that he had to guide his steps by dragging his whip along the low bushes in advance of the hedgerow. He must soon, he thought, be getting near the opening at the stone pit; he should find it out by the break in the hedgerow. He found it out, however, by another circumstance which he had not expected—namely, by certain gleams of light, which he presently guessed to proceed from Silas Marner's cottage.

That cottage and the money hidden within it had been in his mind continually during his walk, and he had been imagining ways of cajoling and tempting the weaver to part with the immediate possession of his money for the sake of receiving interest. Dunstan felt as if there must be a little frightening added to the cajolery, for his own arithmetical convictions were not clear enough to afford him any forcible demonstration as to the advantages of interest. As for security, he regarded it vaguely as a means of cheating a man by making him believe that he would be paid. Altogether, the operation on the miser's mind was a task that

Godfrey would be sure to hand over to his more daring and cunning brother; Dunstan had made up his mind to that; and by the time he saw the light gleaming through the chinks of Marner's shutters, the idea of a dialogue with the weaver had become so familiar to him that it occurred to him as quite a natural thing to make the acquaintance forthwith.

There might be several conveniences attending this course; the weaver had possibly got a lantern, and Dunstan was tired of feeling his way. He was still nearly three-quarters of a mile from home, and the lane was becoming unpleasantly slippery, for the mist was passing into rain. He turned up the bank, not without some fear lest he might miss the right way, since he was not certain whether the light were in front or on the side of the cottage; but he felt the ground before him cautiously with his whip handle, and at last arrived safely at the door. He knocked loudly, rather enjoying the idea that the old fellow would be frightened at the sudden noise. He heard no movement in reply; all was silence in the cottage. Was the weaver gone to bed, then? If so, why had he left a light? That was a strange forgetfulness in the miser. Dunstan knocked still more loudly, and, without pausing for a reply, pushed his fingers through the latchhole, intending to shake the door and pull the latchstring up and down, not doubting that the door was fastened. To his surprise, at this double motion the door opened, and he found himself in front of a bright fire which lit up every corner of the cottage—the bed, the loom, the three chairs, and the table—and showed him that Marner was not there.

Nothing at that moment could be much more inviting to Dunsey than the bright fire on the brick hearth. He walked in and seated himself by it at once. There was something in front of the fire, too, that would have been inviting to a hungry man if it had been in a different stage of cooking. It was a small bit of pork suspended from the kettle-hanger by a string passed through a large door key, in a way known to primitive housekeepers unpossessed of jacks. But the pork had been hung at the farthest extremity of the hanger, apparently to prevent the roasting from proceeding too rapidly during the owner's absence. The old staring simpleton had hot meat for his supper, then, thought Dunstan. People had always said he lived on moldy bread, on purpose to check his appetite. But where could he be at this time, and on such an evening, leaving his supper in this stage of preparation and his door unfastened? Dunstan's own recent difficulty in making his way suggested to him that the weaver had perhaps gone outside his cottage to fetch in fuel, or for some such brief purpose, and had slipped into the stone pit nearby. That was an interesting idea to Dunstan, carrying consequences of entire novelty. If the weaver were dead, who had a right to his money? Who would know where his money was hidden? *Who would know that anybody had come to take it away?* He went no farther into the subtleties of evidence. The pressing question, "Where *is* the money?" now took such entire possession of him as to make him quite forget that the weaver's death was not a certainty. A dull mind, once arriving at an inference that flatters a desire, is rarely able to retain the impression that the notion from which the inference started was purely problematic. Dunstan's mind was as dull as the mind of a possible felon usually is. There were only three hiding places where he had ever heard of cottagers' hoards being found: the thatch, the bed, and a hole in the floor. Marner's cottage had no thatch; and Dunstan's first act, after a train of thought made rapid by the stimulus of cupidity, was to go up to the bed; but while he did so, his eyes traveled eagerly over the floor, where the bricks, distinct in the firelight, were discernable under the sprinkling of sand. There was one spot, and one only, that was quite covered with sand, and sand showing the marks of fingers that had apparently been careful to spread it over a given space. It was near the treadles of the loom. In an instant Dunstan darted to that spot, swept away the sand with his whip, and, inserting the thin end of the hook between the bricks, found that they were loose. In haste he lifted up two bricks and saw what he had no doubt was the object of his search; for what could there be but money in those two leathern bags?

From their weight, they must be filled with guineas. Dunstan felt round the hole to be certain that it held no more; then hastily replaced the bricks and spread the sand over them. Hardly more than five minutes had passed since he entered the cottage, but it seemed to Dunstan like a long while; and though he was without any distinct recognition of the possibility that Marner might be alive and might reenter the cottage at any moment, he felt an undefinable dread laying hold on him as he rose to his feet with the bags in his hand. He would hasten out into the darkness and then consider what he should do with the bags. He closed the door behind him immediately so that he might shut in the stream of light. A few steps would be enough to carry him beyond betrayal by the gleams from the shutter chinks and the latchhole. The rain and darkness had gotten thicker, and he was glad of it. It was awkward walking with both hands filled so that it was as much as he could do to grasp his whip along with one of the bags. But when he had gone a yard or two, he might take his time; so he stepped forward into the darkness.

Chapter 5

When Dunstan Cass turned his back on the cottage, Silas Marner was not more than a hundred yards away from it, plodding along from the village with a sack thrown round his shoulders as an overcoat, and with a horn lantern in his hand. His legs were weary, but his mind was at ease and free from the presentiment of change. He was thinking with double complacency of his supper: first, because it would be hot and savory; and secondly, because it would cost him nothing. For the little bit of pork was a present from that excellent housewife, Miss Priscilla Lammeter, to whom he had this day carried home a handsome piece of linen; and it was only on occasion of a present like this that Silas indulged himself with roast meat. Supper was his favorite meal because it came at his time of revelry when his heart warmed over his gold; whenever he had roast meat, he always chose to have it for supper. But this evening he had no sooner ingeniously knotted his string fast round his bit of pork, twisted the string according to rule over his door key, passed it through the handle and made it fast on the hanger, than he remembered that a piece of very fine twine was indispensable to his "setting up" a new piece of work in his loom early in the morning. It had slipped his memory because, in coming from Mr. Lammeter's, he had not had to pass through the village; but to lose time by going on errands in the morning was out of the question. It was a nasty fog to turn out into, but there were things Silas loved better than his own comfort; so, drawing his pork to the extremity of the hanger, and arming himself with his lantern and his old sack, he set out on what, in ordinary weather, would have been a twenty minutes' errand. He could not have locked his door without undoing his well-knotted string and retarding his supper; it was not worth his while to make that sacrifice. What thief would find his way to Stone Pit on such a night as this? And why should he come on this particular night when he had never come through all the fifteen years before? These questions were not distinctly present in Silas's mind; they merely served to represent the vaguely felt foundation of his freedom from anxiety.

He reached his door in much satisfaction that his errand was done; he opened it, and to his shortsighted eyes everything remained as he had left it, except that the fire sent out a welcome increase of heat. He trod about the floor while putting by his lantern and throwing aside his hat and sack, which merged the marks of Dunstan's feet on the sand in the marks of his own nailed boots. Then he moved his pork nearer to the fire and sat down to the agreeable business of tending the meat and warming himself at the same time.

As soon as he was warm he began to think it would be a long while to wait till after supper before he drew out his guineas, and it would be pleasant to see them on the table before him as he ate his unwonted feast.

He rose and placed his candle unsuspectingly on the floor near his loom, swept away the sand without noticing any change, and removed the bricks. The sight of the empty hole made his heart leap violently, but the belief that his gold was gone could not come at once—only terror and the eager effort to put an end to the terror. He passed his trembling hand all about the hole, trying to think it possible that his eyes had deceived him. Then he held the candle in the hole and examined it curiously, trembling more and more. At last he shook so violently that he let fall the candle and lifted his hands to his head, trying to steady himself, that he might think. Had he put his gold somewhere else, by a sudden resolution last night, and then forgotten it? A

49

man falling into dark waters seeks a momentary footing even on sliding stones; and Silas, by acting as if he believed in false hopes, warded off the moment of despair. He searched in every corner, he turned his bed over, and shook it, and kneaded it; he looked in his brick oven where he laid his sticks. When there was no other place to be searched, he kneeled down again and felt once more all round the hole. There was no untried refuge left for a moment's shelter from the terrible truth.

Yes, there was a sort of refuge which always comes with the prostration of thought under an overpowering passion. It was that expectation of impossibilities, that belief in contradictory images, which is still distinct from madness because it is capable of being dissipated by the external fact. Silas got up from his knees, trembling, and looked around at the table; didn't the gold lie there after all? The table was bare. Then he turned and looked behind him—looked all round his dwelling, seeming to strain his brown eyes after some possible appearance of the bags where he had already sought them in vain. He could see every object in his cottage—and his gold was not there.

Again he put his trembling hands to his head and gave a wild ringing scream, the cry of desolation. For a few moments after, he stood motionless; but the cry had relieved him from the first maddening pressure of the truth. He turned and tottered toward his loom and got into the seat where he worked, instinctively seeking this as the strongest assurance of reality.

And now that all the false hopes had vanished and the first shock of certainty was past, the idea of a thief began to present itself, and he entertained it eagerly because a thief might be caught and made to restore the gold. The thought brought some new strength with it, and he started from his loom to the door. As he opened it, the rain beat in upon him, for it was falling more and more heavily. There were no footsteps to be tracked on such a night—footsteps? When had the thief come? During Silas's absence in the daytime, the door had been locked, and there had been no marks of any inroad on his return by daylight. And in the evening too, he said to himself that everything was the same as when he had left it. The sand and bricks looked as if they had not been moved. *Was* it a thief who had taken the bags? or was it a cruel power that no hands could reach which had delighted in making him a second time desolate? He shrank from this vaguer dread and fixed his mind with struggling effort on the robber with hands, who could be reached by hands. His thoughts glanced at all the neighbors who had made any remarks or asked any questions that he might now regard as a ground of suspicion. There was Jem Rodney, a known poacher, and otherwise disreputable. He had often met Marner in his journeys across the fields and had said something jestingly about the weaver's money; nay, he had once irritated Marner by lingering at the fire instead of going about his business. Jem Rodney was the man—there was ease in the thought. Jem could be found and made to restore the money; Marner did not wish to punish him, but only to get back his gold, which had gone from him and left his soul like a forlorn traveler on an unknown desert. The robber must be laid hold of. Marner's ideas of legal authority were confused, but he felt that he must go and proclaim his loss. The great people in the village—the clergyman, the constable, and Squire Cass—would make Jem Rodney, or somebody else, deliver up the stolen money. He rushed out in the rain under the stimulus of this hope, forgetting to cover his head, not caring to fasten his door; for he felt as if he had nothing left to lose. He ran swiftly, till want of breath compelled him to slacken his pace as he was entering the village at the turning close to the Rainbow.

The Rainbow, in Marner's view, was a place of luxurious resort for rich and stout husbands whose wives had superfluous stores of linen; it was the place where he was likely to find the powers and dignities of Raveloe and where he could most speedily make his loss public. He lifted the latch and turned into the bright kitchen on the right hand, where the less lofty customers of the house were in the habit of assembling, the parlor on the left being reserved for the more select society in which Squire Cass frequently enjoyed the double pleasure of conviviality and condescension. But the parlor was dark tonight, the chief personages who ornamented its circle being all at Mrs. Osgood's birthday party, as Godfrey Cass was. And in consequence of this, the gathering on the high-screened seats in the kitchen was more numerous than usual. Several personages, who would otherwise have been admitted into the parlor and enlarged the opportunity of hectoring and condescension for their betters, being content this evening to vary their enjoyment where they could hector and condescend in a welcoming company.

Chapter 6

The conversation, which was at a high pitch of animation when Silas approached the door of the Rainbow, had, as usual, been slow and intermittent when the company first assembled. There they gathered in a silence which had an air of severity; the more important customers sat nearest the fire, staring at each other. Others, chiefly men in fustian jackets and smock frocks, kept their eyelids down and rubbed their hands across their mouths with embarrassing sadness. At last, Mr. Snell, the landlord, a man of a neutral disposition, accustomed to stand aloof from human differences, broke silence by saying in a doubtful tone to his cousin the butcher—

"Some folks 'ud say that was a fine beast you druv in yesterday, Bob?"

The butcher, a jolly, smiling, red-haired man, was not disposed to answer rashly. He paused and replied, "And they wouldn't be fur wrong, John."

After this feeble, delusive thaw, the silence set in as severely as before.

"Was it a red Durham?" said the farrier, taking up the thread of discourse after the lapse of a few minutes.

The farrier looked at the landlord, and the landlord looked at the butcher, as the person who must take the responsibility of answering.

"Red it was," said the butcher in his good-humored, husky treble, "and a Durham it was."

"Then you needn't tell *me* who you bought it of," said the farrier, looking round with some triumph. "I know who it is has got the red Durhams o' this countryside. And she'd a white star on her brow?" The farrier leaned forward with his hands on his knees as he put this question, and his eyes twinkled knowingly.

"Well, yes—she might," said the butcher slowly, considering that he was giving a decided affirmative. "I don't say contrairy."

"I knew that very well," said the farrier, throwing himself backward again and speaking defiantly. "If *I* don't know Mr. Lammeter's cows, I should like to know who does—that's all. And as for the cow you've bought, bargain or no bargain, I've been at the drenching of her—contradick me who will."

The farrier looked fierce, and the mild butcher's conversational spirit was aroused a little.

"I'm not for contradicking no man," he said; "I'm for peace and quietness. Some are for cutting long ribs—I'm for cutting 'em short myself; but *I* don't quarrel with 'em. All I say is, it's a lovely carcase—and anybody as was reasonable, it 'ud bring tears into their eyes to look at it."

"Well, it's the cow I drenched, whatever it is," pursued the farrier angrily; "and it was Mr. Lammeter's cow, else you told a lie when you said it was a red Durham."

"I tell no lies," said the butcher, with the same mild huskiness as before, "and I contradick none; he's no meat o' mine, nor none o' my bargains. All I say is, it's a lovely carcase. And what I say I'll stick to; but I'll quarrel wi' no man."

"No," said the farrier with bitter sarcasm, looking at the company generally; "and p'rhaps you didn't say the cow was a red Durham; and p'rhaps you didn't say she'd got a star on her brow—stick to that, now you're at it."

"Come, come," said the landlord: "let the cow alone. The truth lies atween you; you're both right and both wrong, as I allays say. And as for the cow's being Mr. Lammeter's, I say nothing to that; but this I say, as the Rainbow's the Rainbow. And for the matter o' that, if the talk is to be o' the Lammeters, *you* know the most upo' that head, eh, Mr. Macey? You remember when first Mr. Lammeter's father come into these parts and took The Warrens?"

Mr. Macey, tailor and parish clerk, the latter of which functions rheumatism had of late obliged him to share with a small-featured young man who sat opposite him, held his white head on one side and twirled his thumbs with an air of complacency, slightly seasoned with criticism.

"I should think I did," said the old man, "and a fine old gentleman he was—as fine and finer nor the Mr. Lammeter as now is. He came from a bit north'ard, so far as I could ever make out, but there's nobody rightly knows about those parts. Only it couldn't be far north'ard, nor much different from this country, for he brought a fine breed o' sheep with him, so there must be pastures there and everything reasonable. We heared tell as he'd sold his own land to come and take The Warrens, and that seemed odd for a man as had land of his own, to come and rent a farm in a strange place. They said it was along of his wife's dying; though there's reasons in things as nobody knows on. That's pretty much what I've made out; yet some folks are so wise they'll find you fifty reasons straight off, and all the while the real reason's winking at 'em in the corner, and they niver see't. Howsomever, it was soon seen as we'd got a new parish'ner as know'd the rights and customs o' things, and kep' a good house, and was well looked on by everybody. The young man—that's the Mr. Lammeter as now is, for he'd niver a sister—soon begun to court Miss Osgood, that's the sister o' the Mr. Osgood as now is, and a fine handsome lass she was—eh, you can't think—they pretend this young lass is like her, but that's the way wi' people as don't know what come before 'em. *I* should know, for I helped the old rector, Mr. Drumlow as was. I helped him marry 'em."

Here Mr. Macey paused. He always gave his narrative in installments, expecting to be questioned according to precedent.

"Ay, and a partic'lar thing happened, didn't it, Mr. Macey, so as you were likely to remember that marriage?" said the landlord in a congratulatory tone.

"I should think there did—a *very* partic'lar thing," said Mr. Macey, nodding sideways. "For Mr. Drumlow— poor old gentleman, I was fond on him, though he'd got a bit confused in his head, what wi' age and wi' taking a drop o' summat warm when the service come of a cold morning. And young Mr. Lammeter he'd have no way but he must be married in Janiwary, which, to be sure, 's a' unreasonable time to be married in, for it isn't like a christening or a burying, as you can't help; and so Mr. Drumlow—poor old gentleman, I was fond on him—but when he come to put the questions, he put 'em by the rule o' contrairy, like, and he says, 'Wilt thou have this man to be thy wedded wife?' says he, and then he says, 'Wilt thou have this woman to thy wedded husband?' says he. But the partic'larest thing of all is as nobody took any notice on it but me, and they answered straight off 'Yes,' like as if it had been me saying 'Amen' i' the right place without listening to what went before."

"But *you* knew what was going on well enough, didn't you, Mr. Macey? You were live enough, eh?" said the butcher.

"Lor' bless you!" said Mr. Macey, pausing, and smiling in pity at the impotence of his hearer's imagination. "Why, I was all of a tremble; it was as if I'd been a coat pulled by the two tails, like; for I couldn't stop the parson, I couldn't take upon me to do that; and yet I said to myself, I says, 'Suppose they shouldn't be fast married, 'cause the words are contrairy?' and my head went working like a mill, for I was allays uncommon for turning things over and seeing all round 'em; and I says to myself, 'Is't the meanin' or the words as makes folks fast i' wedlock?' For the parson meant right, and the bride and bridegroom meant right. But then, when I come to think on it, meanin' goes but a little way i' most things, for you may mean to stick things together and your glue may be bad, and then where are you? And so I says to mysen, 'It isn't the meanin', it's the glue.' And I was worreted as if I'd got three bells to pull at once when we went into the vestry and they begun to sign their names. But where's the use o' talking? You can't think what goes on in 'cute man's inside."

"But you held in for all that, didn't you, Mr. Macey?" said the landlord.

"Ay, I held in tight till I was by mysen wi' Mr. Drumlow, and then I out wi' everything, but respectful, as I allays did. And he made light on it, and he says, 'Pooh, pooh, Macey, make yourself easy,' he says; 'it's neither the meaning nor the words. It's the regester does it. That's the glue.' So you see he settled it easy; for parsons and doctors know everything by heart, like, so as they aren't worreted wi' thinking what's the rights and wrongs o' things, as I'n been many and many's the time. And sure enough the wedding turned out all right, on'y poor Mrs. Lammeter—that's Miss Osgood as was—died afore the lasses was growed up; but for the prosperity and everything respectable, there's no family more looked on."

Every one of Mr. Macey's audience had heard this story many times, but it was listened to as if it had been a favorite tune, and at certain points even breathing was momentarily suspended that the listeners might give their whole minds to the expected words. But there was more to come; and Mr. Snell, the landlord, duly put the leading question.

"Why, old Mr. Lammeter had a pretty fortin, didn't they say, when he come into these parts?"

"Well, yes," said Mr. Macey; "but I dare say it's as much as this Mr. Lammeter's done to keep it whole. For there was allays a talk as nobody could get rich on The Warrens; though he holds it cheap, for it's what they call charity land."

"Ay, and there's few folks know so well as you how it come to be charity land, eh, Mr. Macey?" said the butcher.

"How should they?" said the old clerk, with some contempt. "Why, my grandfather made the grooms' livery for that Mr. Cliff as came and built the big stables at The Warrens. Why, they're stables four times as big as Squire Cass's, for he thought o' nothing but hosses and hunting, Cliff didn't—a London tailor, some folks said, as had gone mad wi' cheating. For he couldn't ride; Lor' bless you! they said he'd got no more grip o' the hoss than if his legs had been cross sticks; my grandfather heard old Squire Cass say so many and many a time. But ride he would as if Old Harry had been a-driving him; and he'd a son, a lad o' sixteen; and nothing would his father have him do, but he must ride and ride—though the lad was frighted, they said. And it was a common saying as the father wanted to ride the tailor out o' the lad and make a gentleman on him—not but what I'm a tailor myself, but in respect as God made me such, I'm proud on it, for MACEY, TAILOR's been wrote up over our door since afore the Queen's heads went out on the shillings. But Cliff, he was ashamed o' being called a tailor, and he was sore vexed as his riding was laughed at, and nobody o' the gentlefolks hereabout could abide him.

Howsomever, the poor lad got sickly and died, and the father didn't live long after him, for he got queerer nor ever, and they said he used to go out i' the dead o' the night wi' a lantern in his hand to the stables and set a lot o' lights burning, for he got as he couldn't sleep; and there he'd stand, cracking his whip and looking at his hosses. They said it was a mercy as the stables didn't get burnt down. But at last he died raving, and they found as he'd left all his property, The Warrens and all, to a London charity. That's how The Warrens come to be charity land. Though, as for the stables, Mr. Lammeter never uses 'em—they're out o' all charicter—Lor' bless you! If you was to set the doors a-banging in 'em, it 'ud sound like thunder half o'er the parish."

"Ay, but there's more going on in the stables than what folks see by daylight, eh, Mr. Macey?" said the landlord.

"Ay, ay; go that way of a dark night, that's all," said Mr. Macey, winking mysteriously, "and then make believe, if you like, as you didn't see lights i' the stables, nor hear the stamping o' the hosses, nor the cracking o' the whips, and howling, too, if it's tow'rt daybreak. 'Cliff's Holiday' has been the name of it ever sin' I were a boy; that's to say, some said it was the holiday Old Harry gev him from roasting like."

"What do you say to that, eh, Dowlas?" said the landlord, turning to the farrier, who was swelling with impatience for his cue. "There's a nut for *you* to crack."

Mr. Dowlas was the negative spirit in the company and was proud of his position.

"Say? I say what a man *should* say as doesn't shut his eyes to look at a finger post. I say, as I'm ready to give any man ten pound, if he'll stand out wi' me any dry night in the pasture before The Warrens stables, as

59

we shall neither see lights nor hear noises, if it isn't the blowing of our own noses. That's what I say, and I've said it many a time; but there's nobody'll ventur a ten-pun' note on their ghos'es as they make so sure of."

"Why, Dowlas, that's easy to say, that is," said Ben Winthrop. "You might as well tell a man as he wouldn't catch the rheumatism if he stood up to 's neck in the pool of a frosty night. It 'ud be fine fun for a man to gain ten pound as he'd catch the rheumatism. Folks as believe in Cliff's Holiday aren't a-going to venture near it for a matter o' ten pound."

"If Master Dowlas wants to know the truth on it," said Mr. Macey with a sarcastic smile, tapping his thumbs together, "he's no call to part with a ten-pun' note—let him go and stan' by himself—there's nobody'll hinder him; and then he can let the parish'ners know if they're wrong."

"Thank you! I'm obliged to you," said the farrier, with a snort of scorn. "If folks are fools, it's no business o' mine. *I* don't want to make out the truth about ghos'es; I know it a'ready. But I'm not against a bet—everything fair and open. Let any man give me ten pound as I shall see Cliff's Holiday, and I'll go and stand by myself. I want no company."

"Ah, but who's to watch you, Dowlas, and see you do it? That's no fair bet," said the butcher.

"No fair?" replied Mr. Dowlas angrily. "I should like to hear any man stand up and say I want to be unfair. Come now, Master Lundy, I should like to hear you say it."

"Very like you would," said the butcher. "But it's no business o' mine. You're none o' my bargains, and I aren't a-going to try and 'bate your price. If anybody'll bid for you, let him. I'm for peace and quietness, I am."

"Yes, that's what every yapping cur is, when you hold a stick up at him," said the farrier. "But I'm afraid o' neither man nor ghost, and *I* aren't a turntail cur."

"Ay, but there's this in it, Dowlas," said the landlord, speaking in a tone of much candor and tolerance. "There's folks, i' my opinion, they can't see ghos'es, not if they stood as plain as a pikestaff before 'em. And there's reason i' that. For there's my wife, now, can't smell, not if she'd the strongest o' cheese under her nose. I never see'd a ghost myself; but then I says to myself, 'Very like I haven't got the smell for 'em.' I mean, putting a ghost for a smell, or else contrairiways. And so, I'm for holding with both sides; for, as I say, the truth lies between 'em. And if Dowlas was to go and stand and say he'd never seen a wink o' Cliff's Holiday all the night through, I'd back him; and if anybody said as Cliff's Holiday was certain sure for all that, I'd back *him* too. For the smell's what I go by."

The landlord's analogical argument was not well received by the farrier—a man intensely opposed to compromise.

"Tut, tut," he said, setting down his glass with refreshed irritation; "what's the smell got to do with it? Did ever a ghost give a man a black eye? That's what I should like to know. If ghos'es want me to believe in 'em, let 'em leave off skulking i' the dark and i' lone places. Let 'em come where there's company and candles."

"As if ghos'es 'ud want to be believed in by anybody so ignirant!" said Mr. Macey, in deep disgust at the farrier's crass incompetence to apprehend the conditions of ghostly phenomena.

Chapter 7

Yet the next moment there seemed to be some evidence that ghosts had a more condescending disposition than Mr. Macey attributed to them; for the pale, thin figure of Silas Marner was suddenly seen standing in the warm light, uttering no word, but looking round at the company with his strange, unearthly eyes. They gave a simultaneous movement like startled insects, and every man present, not excepting even the skeptical farrier, had an impression that he saw, not Silas Marner in the flesh, but an apparition; for the door by which Silas had entered was hidden by the high-screened seats, and no one had noticed his approach.

For a few moments there was a dead silence, Marner's want of breath and agitation not allowing him to speak. The landlord, under the habitual sense that he was bound to keep his house open to all company, and confident in the protection of his unbroken neutrality, at last took on himself the task of adjuring the ghost.

"Master Marner," he said in a conciliatory tone, "what's lacking to you? What's your business here?"

"Robbed!" said Silas gaspingly. "I've been robbed! I want the constable—and the Justice—and Squire Cass—and Mr. Crackenthorp."

"Lay hold on him, Jem Rodney," said the landlord as the idea of a ghost subsided, "He's off his head, I doubt. He's wet through."

Jem Rodney was the outermost man, and sat conveniently near Marner's standing place; but he declined to give his services.

"Come and lay hold on him yourself, Mr. Snell, if you've a mind," said Jem rather sullenly. "He's been robbed, and murdered, too, for what I know," he added, in a muttering tone.

"Jem Rodney!" said Silas, turning and fixing his strange eyes on the suspected man.

"Ay, Master Marner, what do ye want wi' me?" said Jem, trembling a little, and seizing his cup as a defensive weapon.

"If it was you stole my money," said Silas, clasping his hands entreatingly and raising his voice to a cry, "give it me back and I won't meddle with you. I won't set the constable on you. Give it me back, and I'll let you . . . I'll let you have a guinea."

"Me stole your money!" said Jem angrily. "I'll pitch this cup at your eye if you talk o' *my* stealing your money."

"Come, come, Master Marner," said the landlord, now rising resolutely and seizing Marner by the shoulder, "if you've got any information to lay, speak it out sensible, and show as you're in your right mind if you expect anybody to listen to you. You're as wet as a drownded rat. Sit down and dry yourself, and speak straight forrard."

"Ah, to be sure, man," said the farrier, who began to feel that he had not been quite on a par with himself and the occasion. "Let's have no more staring and screaming, else we'll have you strapped for a madman. That was why I didn't speak at the first—thinks I, the man's run mad."

"Ay, ay, make him sit down," said several voices at once, well pleased that the reality of ghosts remained still an open question.

The landlord forced Marner to take off his coat and then to sit down on a chair aloof from everyone else, in the center of the circle and in the direct rays of the fire. The weaver, too feeble to have any distinct purpose beyond that of getting help to recover his money, submitted unresistingly. The transient fears of the company were now forgotten in their strong curiosity, and all faces were turned toward Silas, when the landlord, having seated himself again, said:

"Now then, Master Marner, what's this you've got to say—as you've been robbed? Speak out."

"He'd better not say again as it was me robbed him," cried Jem Rodney hastily. "What could I ha' done with his money? I could as easy steal the parson's surplice and wear it."

"Hold your tongue, Jem, and let's hear what he's got to say," said the landlord. "Now then, Master Marner."

Silas now told his story, under frequent questioning as the mysterious character of the robbery became evident.

This strangely novel situation of opening his trouble to his Raveloe neighbors, of sitting in the warmth of a hearth not his own, and feeling the presence of faces and voices that were his nearest promise of help, had doubtless its influence on Marner in spite of his passionate preoccupation with his loss. Our consciousness rarely registers the beginning of a growth within us any more than without us; there have been many circulations of the sap before we detect the smallest sign of the bud.

The slight suspicion with which his hearers at first listened to him gradually melted away before the convincing simplicity of his distress. It was impossible for the neighbors to doubt that Marner was telling the truth.

"It isn't Jem Rodney as has done this work, Master Marner," said the landlord. "You mustn't be a-casting your eye at poor Jem. There may be a bit of a reckoning against Jem for the matter of a hare or so if anybody was bound to keep their eyes staring open and niver to wink; but Jem's been a-sitting here, like the decentest man i' the parish, since before you left your house, Master Marner, by your own account."

"Ay, ay," said Mr. Macey. "Let's have no accusing o' the innicent. That isn't the law. There must be folks to swear again' a man before he can be ta'en up. Let's have no accusing of the innicent, Master Marner."

Memory was not so utterly torpid in Silas that it could not be wakened by these words. With a movement of compunction as new and strange to him as everything else within the last hour, he started from his chair and went close up to Jem, looking at him as if he wanted to assure himself of the expression in his face.

"I was wrong," he said. "Yes, yes, I ought to have thought. There's nothing to witness against you, Jem. Only you'd been into my house oftener than anybody else, and so you came into my head. I don't accuse you. I won't accuse anybody. Only," he added, lifting up his hands to his head and turning away with bewildered misery, "I try . . . I try to think where my guineas can be."

"Ay, ay, they're gone where it's hot enough to melt 'em, I doubt," said Mr. Macey.

"Tchuh!" said the farrier. And then he asked, with a cross-examining air, "How much money might there be in the bags, Master Marner?"

"Two hundred and seventy-two pounds, twelve and sixpence, last night when I counted it," said Silas, seating himself again with a groan.

"Pooh! Why, they'd be none so heavy to carry. Some tramp's been in, that's all; and as for the no footmarks and the bricks and the sand being all right—why, your eyes are pretty much like a insect's, Master Marner. They're obliged to look so close you can't see much at a time. It's my opinion as, if I'd been you, or you'd been me—for it comes to the same thing—you wouldn't have thought you'd found everything as you left it. But what I vote is, as two of the sensiblest o' the company should go with you to Master Kench, the constable's— he's ill i' bed, I know that much—and get him to appoint one of us his deppity; for that's the law, and I don't think anybody'll take upon him to contradick me there. It isn't much of a walk to Kench's; and then, if it's me as is deppity, I'll go back with you, Master Marner, and examine your premises; and if anybody's got any fault to find with that, I'll thank him to stand up and say it out like a man."

By this speech the farrier had reestablished his self-complacency, and waited with confidence to hear himself named as one of the superlatively sensible men.

"Let us see how the night is, though," said the landlord, who also considered himself personally concerned in this proposition. "Why, it rains heavy still," he said, returning from the door.

"Well, I'm not the man to be afraid o' the rain," said the farrier. "For it'll look bad when Justice Malam hears as respectable men like us had information laid before 'em and took no steps."

The landlord agreed with this view, and after taking the sense of the company, he consented to take on himself the chill dignity of going to Kench's. But to the farrier's strong disgust, Mr. Macey now started an objection to his proposing himself as a deputy constable; for that oracular old gentleman, claiming to know the law, stated, as a fact delivered to him by his father, that no doctor could be a constable.

"And you're a doctor, I reckon, though you're only a cow doctor, for a fly's a fly, though it may be a hoss fly," concluded Mr. Macey, wondering a little at his own "cuteness."

There was a hot debate upon this, the farrier being of course indisposed to renounce the quality of doctor, but contending that a doctor could be a constable if he liked—the law meant he needn't be one if he didn't like. Mr. Macey thought this was nonsense, since the law was not likely to be fonder of doctors than of other folks. Moreover, if it was in the nature of doctors more than of other men not to like being constables, how came Mr. Dowlas to be so eager to act in that capacity?

"*I* don't want to act the constable," said the farrier, driven into a corner by this merciless reasoning; "and there's no man can say it of me, if he'd tell the truth. But if there's to be any jealousy and envying about going to Kench's in the rain, let them go as like it. You won't get me to go, I can tell you."

By the landlord's intervention, however, the dispute was accommodated. Mr. Dowlas consented to go as a second person disinclined to act officially; and so poor Silas, furnished with some old coverings, turned out with his two companions into the rain again, thinking of the long night hours before him, not as those do who long to rest, but as those who expect to "watch for the morning."

Chapter 8

When Godfrey Cass returned from Mrs. Osgood's party at midnight, he was not much surprised to learn that Dunsey had not come home. Perhaps he had not sold Wildfire and was waiting for another chance. Perhaps, on that foggy afternoon, he had preferred housing himself at the Red Lion at Batherley for the night, if the run had kept him in that neighborhood; for he was not likely to feel much concern about leaving his brother in suspense. Godfrey's mind was too full of Nancy Lammeter's looks and behavior, too full of the exasperation against himself and his lot, which the sight of her always produced in him, for him to give much thought to Wildfire, or to the probabilities of Dunstan's conduct.

The next morning the whole village was excited by the story of the robbery, and Godfrey, like everyone else, was occupied in gathering and discussing news about it, and in visiting Stone Pit. The rain had washed away all possibility of distinguishing footmarks, but a close investigation of the spot had disclosed, in the direction opposite to the village, a tinderbox, with a flint and steel, half sunk in the mud. It was not Silas's tinderbox, for the only one he had ever had was still standing on his shelf; and the inference generally accepted was that the tinderbox in the ditch was somehow connected with the robbery. A small minority shook their heads and intimated their opinion that it was not a robbery to have much light thrown on it by tinderboxes, that Master Marner's tale had a queer look with it, and that such things had been known as a man's doing himself a mischief and then setting the justice to look for the doer. When questioned closely as to their grounds for this opinion, and what Master Marner had to gain by such false pretenses, they only shook their heads as before and observed that there was no knowing what some folks counted gain; moreover, that everybody had a right to their own opinions, grounds or no grounds, and that the weaver, as everybody knew, was partly crazy. Mr. Macey, though he joined in the defense of Marner against all suspicions of deceit, also pooh-poohed the tinderbox; indeed, repudiated it as a rather impious suggestion and tended to imply that everything must be done by human hands and that there was no power which could make away with the guineas without moving the bricks. Nevertheless, he turned round rather sharply on Mr. Tookey, when the zealous deputy, feeling that this was a view of the case peculiarly suited to a parish clerk, carried it still further, and doubted whether it was right to inquire into a robbery at all when the circumstances were so mysterious.

While these discussions were going on among the group outside the Rainbow, a higher consultation was being carried on within under the presidency of Mr. Crackenthorp, the rector, assisted by Squire Cass and other substantial parishioners. It had just occurred to Mr. Snell, the landlord—he being, as he observed, a man accustomed to put two and two together—to connect with the tinderbox, which, as deputy constable, he himself had had the honorable distinction of finding, certain recollections of a peddler who had called at the house about a month before and had actually stated that he carried a tinderbox about with him. Here, surely, was a clue to be followed out. Mr. Snell gradually recovered a vivid impression of the effect produced on him by the peddler's countenance and conversation. He had a "look with his eye" which fell unpleasantly on Mr. Snell's sensitive organism. To be sure, he didn't say anything particular—no, except that about the tinderbox—but it isn't what a man says, it's the way he says it.

Moreover, he had a swarthy foreignness of complexion which boded little honesty.

"Did he wear earrings?" Mr. Crackenthorp wished to know, having some acquaintance with foreign customs.

"Well—stay—let me see," said Mr. Snell. After stretching the corners of his mouth and contracting his eyes, as if he were trying to see the earrings, he appeared to give up the effort, and said, "Well, he'd got earrings in his box to sell, so it's nat'ral to suppose he might wear 'em. But he called at every house, a'most, in the village; there's somebody else, mayhap, saw 'em in his ears, though I can't take upon me rightly to say."

Mr. Snell was correct in his surmise that somebody else would remember the peddler's earrings. For on the spread of inquiry among the villagers it was stated, with gathering emphasis, that the parson had wanted to know whether the peddler wore earrings in his ears, and an impression was created that a great deal depended on the eliciting of this fact. Of course, everyone who heard the question, not having any distinct image of the peddler as *without* earrings, immediately had an image of him *with* earrings, larger or smaller as the case might be; and the image was presently taken for a vivid recollection, so that the glazier's wife, a well-intentioned woman, not given to lying, and whose house was among the cleanest in the village, was ready to declare that she had seen big earrings, in the shape of the young moon, in the peddler's two ears. Jinny Oates, the cobbler's daughter, being a more imaginative person, stated not only that she had seen them too, but that they had made her blood creep, as it did at that very moment while there she stood.

Also, by way of throwing further light on this clue of the tinderbox, a collection was made of all the articles purchased from the peddler and was carried to the Rainbow to be exhibited there. In fact, there was a general feeling in the village that, for the clearing up of this robbery, there must be a great deal done at the Rainbow and that no man need offer his wife an excuse of going there while it was the scene of severe public duties.

Some disappointment was felt, and perhaps a little indignation also, when it became known that Silas Marner, on being questioned by the Squire and the parson, had retained no other recollection of the peddler than that he had called at his door, but had not entered his house, having turned away at once when Silas, holding the door ajar, had said that he wanted nothing. This had been Silas's testimony, though he clutched strongly at the idea of the peddler's being the culprit, if only because it gave him a definite image of a whereabout for his gold after it had been taken away from its hiding place. He could see it now in the peddler's box. It was observed, with some irritation in the village, that anybody but a "blind creatur" like Marner would have seen the man prowling about; for how came he to leave his tinderbox in the ditch close by, if he hadn't been lingering there? Doubtless, he had made his observations when he saw Marner at the door. Anybody might know—just looking at him—that the weaver was a half-crazy miser. It was a wonder the peddler hadn't murdered him; men of that sort, with rings in their ears, had been known for murderers often and often. There had been one tried at court sessions not so long ago, and there were people living who remembered it.

Godfrey Cass, indeed, entering the Rainbow during one of Mr. Snell's frequently repeated recitals of his testimony, had treated it lightly, stating that he himself had bought a penknife of the peddler and thought him a merry, grinning fellow enough. It was all nonsense, he said, about the man's evil looks. But this was spoken of

71

in the village as the random talk of youth, "as if it was only Mr. Snell who had seen something odd about the peddler!" On the contrary, there were at least half a dozen who were ready to go before Justice Malam and give in much more striking testimony than any the landlord could furnish. It was to be hoped Mr. Godfrey would not go to Tarley and throw cold water on what Mr. Snell said there and so prevent the justice from drawing up a warrant. He was suspected of intending this when, after midday, he was seen setting off on horseback in the direction of Tarley.

By this time Godfrey's interest in the robbery had faded before his growing anxiety about Dunstan and Wildfire, and he was going, not to Tarley, but to Batherley, unable to rest in uncertainty about them any longer. The possibility that Dunstan had played him the ugly trick of riding away with Wildfire, planning to return at the end of a month when he had gambled away or otherwise squandered the price of the horse, was a fear that urged itself upon him more, even, than the thought of an accidental injury. Now that the party at Mrs. Osgood's was past, he was irritated with himself that he had trusted his horse to Dunstan. Instead of trying to still his fears, he encouraged them with that superstitious impression which clings to some that if evil is expected very strongly, it is the less likely to come. When he heard a horse approaching at a trot and saw a hat rising above a hedge beyond an angle of the land, he felt as if his conjuration had succeeded. No sooner did the horse come within sight than his heart sank again. It was not Wildfire; and in a few moments more he discerned that the rider was not Dunstan, but Bryce, who pulled up to speak with a face that implied something disagreeable.

"Well, Mr. Godfrey, that's a lucky brother of yours, that Master Dunsey, isn't he?"

"What do you mean?" said Godfrey hastily.

"Why, hasn't he been home yet?" said Bryce.

"Home? No. What has happened? Be quick. What has he done with my horse?"

"Ah, I thought it was yours, though he pretended you had parted with it to him."

"Has he thrown him down and broken his knees?" said Godfrey, flushed with exasperation.

"Worse than that," said Bryce. "You see, I'd made a bargain with him to buy the horse for a hundred and twenty—a swinging price, because I always liked the horse, and what does he do but go and stake him—fly at a hedge with stakes in it, atop of a bank with a ditch before it. The horse had been dead a pretty good while when he was found. So he hasn't been home since, has he?"

"Home? No," said Godfrey, "and he'd better keep away. I might have known this would be the end of it."

"Well, to tell you the truth," said Bryce, "after I'd bargained for the horse, it did come into my head that he might be riding and selling the horse without your knowledge, for I didn't believe it was his own. I knew Master Dunsey was up to his tricks sometimes, but where can he be gone? He's never been seen at Batherley. He couldn't have been hurt, for he must have walked off."

"Hurt?" said Godfrey bitterly. "He'll never be hurt—he's made to hurt other people."

"So you *did* give him leave to sell the horse, eh?" said Bryce.

"Yes, I wanted to part with the horse. He was always a little too hard in the mouth for me," said Godfrey, his pride making him wince under the idea that Bryce guessed the sale to be a matter of necessity. "I was going to see after him. I thought some mischief had happened. I'll go back now," he added, turning the horse's head and wishing he could get rid of Bryce, for he felt that the long-dreaded crisis in his life was close upon him. "You're coming on to Raveloe, aren't you?"

"Well, no, not now," said Bryce. "I *was* coming round there, for I had to go to Flitton, and I thought I might as well take you in my way and just let you know all I knew myself about the horse. I suppose Master Dunsey didn't like to show himself till the ill news had blown over a bit."

"Perhaps," said Godfrey rather absently. Then rousing himself, he said with an effort at carelessness, "We shall hear of him soon enough, I'll be bound."

"Well, here's my turning," said Bryce, not surprised to perceive that Godfrey was rather "down." "So I'll bid you good day, and wish I may bring you better news another time."

Godfrey rode along slowly, representing to himself the scene of confession to his father, from which he felt there was now no longer any escape. The revelation about the money must be made the very next morning; and if he withheld the rest, Dunstan would be sure to come back shortly, and, finding that he must bear the brunt of his father's anger, would tell the whole story out of spite, even though he had nothing to gain by it. There was one step, perhaps, by which he might still win Dunstan's silence and put off the evil day. He might tell his father that he had himself spent the money paid to him by Fowler; and as he had never been guilty of such an offense before, the affair would blow over after a little storming. But Godfrey could not bend himself to this. He felt that in letting Dunstan have the money, he had already been guilty of a breach of trust hardly less culpable than that of spending the money directly for his own behoof; and yet there was a distinction between the two acts which made him feel that the one was so much more blackening than the other as to be intolerable to him.

"I don't pretend to be a good fellow," he said to himself, "but I'm not a scoundrel—at least I'll stop short somewhere. I'll bear the consequences of what I *have* done sooner than make believe I've done what I never would have done. I'd never have spent the money for my own pleasure. I was tortured into it."

Through the remainder of this day Godfrey, with only occasional fluctuations, kept his will bent in the direction of a complete avowal to his father, and he withheld the story of Wildfire's loss till the next morning so that it might serve him as an introduction to heavier matters. The old Squire was accustomed to his son's frequent absence from home, and thought neither Dunstan's nor Wildfire's nonappearance a matter calling for remark. Godfrey said to himself again and again that if he let slip this one opportunity of confession, he might never have another. The revelation might be made even in a more odious way than by Dunstan's malignity: *she* might come as she had threatened to do. And then he tried to make the scene easier to himself by rehearsal; he made up his mind how he would pass from the admission of his weakness in letting Dunstan have the money to the fact that Dunstan had a hold on him which he had been unable to shake off, and how he would work up his father to expect something very bad before he told him the fact. The old Squire was an implacable man; he made resolutions in violent anger, and he was not to be moved from them after his anger had subsided. Still there was just the chance, Godfrey thought, that his father's pride might see this marriage in a light that would induce him to hush it up, rather than turn his son out and make the family the talk of the country for ten miles around.

This was the view of the case that Godfrey managed to keep before him pretty closely till midnight, and he went to sleep thinking that he was done with inward debating. But when he awoke in the still morning darkness, he found it impossible to reawaken his evening thoughts. It was as if they had been tired out and were not to be roused to further work. Instead of arguments for confession, he could now feel the presence of nothing but its evil consequences. The old dread of disgrace came back—the old shrinking from the thought of raising a hopeless barrier between himself and Nancy and the old disposition to rely on chances which might be favorable to him and save him from betrayal. Why, after all, should he cut off the hope of them by his own act? He had seen the matter in a wrong light yesterday. He had been in a rage with Dunstan and had thought of nothing but a thorough breakup of their mutual understanding; but what would be really wisest for him to do was to try and soften his father's anger against Dunsey and keep things as nearly as possible in their old condition. If Dunsey did not come back for a few days (and Godfrey did not know but that the rascal had enough money in his pocket to enable him to keep away still longer), everything might blow over.

Chapter 9

Godfrey rose and took his breakfast earlier than usual, but lingered in the wainscoted parlor till his younger brothers had finished their meal and gone out; awaiting his father, who always took a walk with his managing man before breakfast. Everyone breakfasted at a different hour in Red House, and the Squire was always the latest, giving a long chance to a rather feeble morning appetite before he tried it. The table had been spread with substantial eatables nearly two hours before he presented himself—a tall, stout man of sixty, with a face in which the knit brow and rather hard glance seemed contradicted by the slack and feeble mouth. His person showed marks of habitual neglect, his dress was slovenly; and yet there was something in the presence of the old Squire distinguishable from that of the ordinary farmers in the parish, who were perhaps every whit as refined as he, but, having slouched their way through life with a consciousness of being in the vicinity of their "betters," wanted that self-possession and authoritativeness of voice and carriage which belonged to a man who thought of superiors as remote existences with whom he had personally little more to do than with America or the stars. The Squire had been used to parish homage all his life, used to the presupposition that his family, his tankards, and everything that was his were the oldest and best; and he never associated with any gentry higher than himself.

He glanced at his son as he entered the room and said, "What, sir! haven't *you* had your breakfast yet?" But there was no pleasant morning greeting between them; not because of any unfriendliness, but because the sweet flower of courtesy is not a growth of such homes as Red House.

"Yes, sir," said Godfrey, "I've had my breakfast, but I was waiting to speak to you."

"Ah! well," said the Squire, throwing himself indifferently into his chair and speaking in a ponderous, coughing fashion—which was felt in Raveloe to be a sort of privilege of his rank—while he cut a piece of beef and held it up before the deerhound that had come in with him. "Ring the bell for my breakfast, will you? You youngsters' business is your own pleasure, mostly. There's no hurry about it for anybody but yourselves."

The Squire's life was quite as idle as his sons', but it was a fiction kept up by himself and his contemporaries in Raveloe that youth was exclusively the period of folly, and that their aged wisdom was constantly in a state of endurance mitigated by sarcasm. Godfrey waited, before he spoke again, until breakfast had been brought and the door closed—an interval during which Fleet, the deerhound, had consumed enough bits of beef to make a poor man's holiday dinner.

"There's been a piece of ill luck with Wildfire," he began. ". . . happened the day before yesterday."

"What! Broke his knees?" said the Squire. "I thought you knew how to ride better than that, sir. I never threw a horse down in my life. If I had, I might ha' whistled for another, for *my* father wasn't quite so ready to unstring as some other fathers I know of. But they must turn over a new leaf. *They* must. What with mortgages and arrears, I'm as short o' cash as a roadside pauper. That fool Kimble says the newspaper's talking about peace. Why, the country wouldn't have a leg to stand on. Prices 'ud run down, and I should never get my arrears, not even if I sold all the fellows up. There's that Fowler, I won't put up with him any longer; I've told Winthrop to go to Cox this very day. The lying scoundrel told me he'd be sure to pay me a hundred last month. He takes advantage because he's on that outlying farm and thinks I shall forget him."

The Squire had delivered this speech in a coughing and interrupted manner, but with no pause long enough for Godfrey to make it a pretext for taking up the word again. He felt that his father meant to ward off any request for money on the ground of the misfortune with Wildfire and that the emphasis he had thus been led to lay on his shortness of cash and his arrears was likely to produce an attitude of mind the utmost unfavorable for his own disclosure. But he must go on, now he had begun.

"It's worse than breaking the horse's knees—he's been staked and killed," he said, as soon as his father was silent and had begun to cut his meat. "I wasn't thinking of asking you to buy me another horse. I was only thinking I'd lost the means of paying you with the price of Wildfire, as I'd meant to do. Dunsey took him to the hunt to sell him for me the other day, and after he'd made a bargain for a hundred and twenty with Bryce, he went after the hounds and took some fool's leap or other that did for the horse at once. If it hadn't been for that, I should have paid you a hundred pounds this morning."

The Squire had laid down his knife and fork and was staring at his son in amazement, not being sufficiently quick of brain to form a probable guess as to what could have caused so strange an inversion of the paternal and filial relations as this proposition of his son to pay him a hundred pounds.

"The truth is, sir—I'm very sorry—I was quite to blame," said Godfrey. "Fowler did pay that hundred pounds. He paid it to me when I was over there one day last month. Dunsey bothered me for the money, and I let him have it because I hoped I should be able to pay it to you before this."

The Squire was purple with anger before his son had done speaking, and found utterance difficult. "You let

Dunsey have it, sir? And how long have you been so thick with Dunsey that you must collogue with him to embezzle my money? Are you turning out a scamp? I tell you I won't have it. I'll turn the whole pack of you out of the house together and marry again. I'd have you to remember, sir, my property's got no entail on it; since my grandfather's time the Casses can do as they like with their land. Remember that, sir. Let Dunsey have the money! Why should you let Dunsey have the money? There's some lie at the bottom of it."

"There's no lie, sir," said Godfrey. "I wouldn't have spent the money myself, but Dunsey bothered me, and I was a fool and let him have it. I meant to pay it, whether he did or not. That's the whole story. I never meant to embezzle money, and I'm not the man to do it. You never knew me to do a dishonest trick, sir."

"Where's Dunsey, then? What do you stand talking there? Go and fetch Dunsey, as I tell you, and let him give account of what he wanted the money for and what he's done with it. He shall repent of it. I'll turn him out. I said I would, and I'll do it. He shan't brave me. Go and fetch him."

"Dunsey isn't come back, sir."

"What! Did he break his own neck then?" said the Squire, with some disgust at the idea that, in that case, he could not fulfill his threat.

"No, he wasn't hurt, I believe, for the horse was found dead, and Dunsey must have walked off. I daresay we shall see him again by and by. I don't know where he is."

"And what must you be letting him have my money for? Answer me that," said the Squire, attacking Godfrey again, since Dunsey was not within reach.

"Well, sir, I don't know," said Godfrey hesitatingly. That was a feeble evasion, but Godfrey was not fond of lying, and, not being sufficiently aware that no sort of duplicity can long flourish without the help of vocal falsehoods, he was quite unprepared with invented motives.

"You don't know? I tell you what it is, sir. You've been up to some trick, and you've been bribing him not to tell," said the Squire, with a sudden acuteness which startled Godfrey. He felt his heart beat violently at the nearness of his father's guess. The sudden alarm pushed him on to take the next step—a very slight impulse suffices for that on a downward road.

"Why, sir," he said, trying to speak with careless ease, "it was a little affair between me and Dunsey; it's no matter to anybody else. It's hardly worthwhile to pry into young men's fooleries; it wouldn't have made any difference to you, sir, if I'd not had the bad luck to lose Wildfire. I should have paid you the money."

"Fooleries! Pshaw! It's time you'd done with fooleries. And I'd have you know, sir, you *must* ha' done with 'em," said the Squire, frowning and casting an angry glance at his son. "Your goings on are not what I shall find money for any longer. There's my grandfather had his stables full o' horses and kept a good house, too, and in worse times by what I can make out; and so might I, if I hadn't four good-for-nothing fellows to hang on me like horseleeches. I've been too good a father to you all—that's what it is. But I shall pull up, sir."

Godfrey was silent. He was not likely to be very penetrating in his judgments, but he had always had a sense that his father's indulgence had not been kindness, and had had a vague longing for some discipline that would have checked his own errant weakness and helped his better will. The Squire ate his bread and meat hastily, then turned his chair from the table and began to speak again.

"It'll be all the worse for you, you know. You should try and help me keep things together."

"Well, sir, I've often offered to take the management of things, but you know you've taken it ill always and seemed to think I wanted to push you out of your place."

"I know nothing o' your offering or o' my taking it ill," said the Squire, whose memory consisted in certain strong impressions unmodified by detail; "but I know one who you seem to be thinking o' marrying, and I don't offer to put any obstacles in your way, as some fathers would. I'd as lief you married Lammeter's daughter as anybody. I suppose, if I'd said you nay, you'd ha' kept on with it; but, for want o' contradiction, you've changed your mind. You're a shilly-shally fellow; you take after your poor mother. She never had a will of her own; a woman has no call for one, if she's got a proper man for her husband. But *your* wife will need one, for you hardly know your own mind enough to make both your legs walk one way. The lass hasn't said downright she won't have you, has she?"

"No," said Godfrey, feeling very hot and uncomfortable; "but I don't think she will."

"Think! Why, haven't you the courage to ask her? Do you stick to it, you want to have *her*—don't you?"

"There's no other woman I want to marry," said Godfrey evasively.

"Well, then, let me make the offer for you if you haven't the pluck to do it yourself. Lammeter isn't likely to be loath for his daughter to marry into *my* family, I should think. As for the pretty lass, she wouldn't have her cousin—and there's nobody else, as I see, could ha' stood in your way."

"I'd rather let it be, please, sir, at present," said Godfrey in alarm. "I think she's a little offended with me just now, and I should like to speak for myself. A man must manage these things for himself."

"Well, speak, then, and manage it, and see if you can't turn over a new leaf. That's what a man must do when he thinks o' marrying."

"I don't see how I can think of it at present, sir. You wouldn't like to settle me on one of the farms, I suppose. I don't think she'd come to live in this house with all my brothers. It's a different sort of life to what she's been used to."

"Not come to live in this house? Don't tell me. You ask her, that's all," said the Squire, with a short, scornful laugh.

"I'd rather let the thing be, at present, sir," said Godfrey. "I hope you won't try to hurry it on by saying anything."

"I shall do what I choose," said the Squire, "and I shall let you know I'm master; else you may turn out, and find an estate to drop into somewhere else. Go out and tell Winthrop not to go to Cox's, but wait for me. Tell 'em to get my horse saddled. And stop, look out, and get that hack o' Dunsey's sold; then hand me the money, will you? He'll keep no more hacks at my expense. If you know where he's sneaking—I daresay you do—you may tell him to spare himself the journey o' coming back home. Let him turn ostler and keep himself. He shan't hang on me any more."

"I don't know where he is; and if I did, it isn't my place to tell him to keep away," said Godfrey, moving toward the door.

"Confound it, sir, don't stay arguing, but go and order my horse," said the Squire.

Godfrey left the room, hardly knowing whether he were more relieved by the sense that the interview was ended without having made any change in his position or more uneasy that he had entangled himself still further in prevarication and deceit. What had passed about his proposing to Nancy had raised a new alarm, lest by some after-dinner words of his father's to Mr. Lammeter, he should be thrown into the embarrassment of being obliged absolutely to decline her when she seemed to be within his reach. He fled to his usual refuge, that of hoping for some unforeseen turn of fortune, some favorable chance which would save him from unpleasant consequences—perhaps even justify his insincerity by manifesting its prudence.

In this point of trusting to some throw of fortune's dice, Godfrey can hardly be called old-fashioned. Favorable Chance is the god of all men who follow their own devices instead of obeying a law they believe in. Let even a polished man of these days get into a position he is ashamed to avow, and his mind will be bent on all the possible issues that may deliver him from the calculable results of that position. Let him live outside his income or shirk the resolute, honest work that brings wages, and he will presently find himself dreaming of a possible benefactor, a possible simpleton who may be cajoled into using his interest, a possible state of mind in some possible person not yet forthcoming. Let him neglect the responsibilities of his office, and he will inevitably anchor himself on the chance that the thing left undone may turn out not to be of the supposed importance. Let him betray his friend's confidence, and he will adore that same cunning complexity called Chance, which gives him the hope that his friend will never know. Let him forsake a decent craft that he may pursue the gentilities of a profession to which nature never called him and his religion will infallibly be the worship of blessed Chance, which he will believe in as the mighty creator of success. The evil principle deprecated in that religion is the orderly sequence by which the seed brings forth a crop after its kind.

Chapter 10

Justice Malam was naturally regarded in Tarley and Raveloe as a man of capacious mind, seeing that he could draw much wider conclusions without evidence than could be expected of his neighbors who were not on the Commission of the Peace. Such a man was not likely to neglect the clue of the tinderbox, and an inquiry was set concerning a peddler, name unknown, with curly black hair and a foreign complexion, carrying a box of cutlery and jewelry and wearing large rings in his ears. But either because inquiry was too slow-footed to overtake him, or because the description applied to so many peddlers that inquiry did not know how to choose among them, weeks passed away, and there was no other result concerning the robbery than a gradual cessation of the excitement it had caused in Raveloe. Dunstan Cass's absence was hardly a subject of remark; he had once before had a quarrel with his father and had gone off, nobody knew whither, to return at the end of six weeks, take up his old quarters unforbidden and swagger as usual. His own family, who equally expected this issue, with the sole difference that the Squire was determined this time to forbid him the old quarters, never mentioned his absence; and when his Uncle Kimble or Mr. Osgood noticed it, the story of his having killed Wildfire and committed some offense against his father was enough to prevent surprise. To connect the fact of Dunsey's disappearance with that of the robbery occurring on the same day lay quite away from the track of everyone's thought—even Godfrey's, who had better reason than anyone else to know what his brother was capable of. He remembered no mention of the weaver between them since the time, twelve years ago, when it was their boyish sport to deride him. Besides, his imagination constantly created an alibi for

Dunstan. He saw him continually in some congenial haunt to which he had walked off on leaving Wildfire—he saw him sponging on chance acquaintances and meditating a return home to the old amusement of tormenting his elder brother.

When the robbery was talked of at the Rainbow and elsewhere in good company, the balance continued to waver between the rational explanation founded on the tinderbox and the theory of an impenetrable mystery that mocked investigation. The advocates of the tinderbox-and-peddler view considered the other side a muddleheaded and credulous set, who, because they themselves were walleyed, supposed everybody else to have the same blank outlook.

While poor Silas's loss served thus to brush the slow current of Raveloe conversation, Silas himself was feeling the withering desolation of that bereavement about which his neighbors were arguing at their ease. To anyone who had observed him before he lost his gold, it might have seemed that so withered and shrunken a life as his could hardly be susceptible of a bruise, could hardly endure any subtraction but such as would put an end to it altogether. In reality it had been an eager life, filled with immediate purpose which fenced him in from the wide, cheerless unknown. It had been a clinging life; and though the object round which its fibers had clung was a dead, disrupted thing, it satisfied the need for clinging. Now the fence was broken down—the support was snatched away. Marner's thoughts could no longer move in their old round and were baffled by a blank like that which meets a plodding ant when the earth has broken away on its homeward path. The loom was there, and the weaving, and the growing pattern in the cloth; but the bright treasure in the hole under his feet was gone; the prospect of handling and counting it was gone; the evening had no phantasm of delight to still the poor soul's craving. The thought of the money he would get by his actual work could bring no joy, for its meager image was only a fresh reminder of his loss; and hope was too heavily crushed by the sudden blow for his imagination to dwell on the growth of a new hoard from that small beginning.

He filled up the blank with grief. As he sat weaving, he every now and then moaned low, like one in pain; it was the sign that his thoughts had come round again to the sudden chasm—to the empty evening time. All the evening, as he sat in his loneliness by his dull fire, he leaned his elbows on his knees, clasped his head with his hands, and moaned very low—not as one who seeks to be heard.

Yet he was not utterly forsaken in his trouble. The repulsion Marner had always created in his neighbors was partly dissipated by the new light in which this misfortune had shown him. Instead of a man who had more cunning than honest folks could come by, and, what was worse, had not the inclination to use that cunning in a neighborly way, it was now apparent that Silas had not cunning enough to keep his own. He was generally spoken of as a "poor mushed creatur"; and that avoidance of his neighbors, which had before been referred to his ill will and to a probable addiction to worse company, was now considered mere craziness.

This change to a kindlier feeling was shown in various ways. The odor of Christmas cooking being on the wind, it was the season when superfluous pork and black puddings are suggestive of charity in well-to-do families; and Silas's misfortune had brought him uppermost in the memory of housekeepers like Mrs. Osgood. Mr. Crackenthorp, too, while he admonished Silas that his money had probably been taken from him because he thought too much of it and never came to church, enforced the doctrine by a present of pigs' pettitoes, well calculated to dissipate unfounded prejudices against the clerical character. Neighbors who had nothing but verbal consolation to give showed a disposition not only to greet Silas and discuss his misfortune at some length when they encountered him in the village, but also to take the trouble of calling at his cottage and getting him to repeat all the details on the very spot; and then they would try to cheer him by saying, "Well, Master Marner, you're no worse off nor other poor folks, after all; and if you was to be crippled, the parish 'ud give you a 'lowance."

I suppose one reason why we are seldom able to comfort our neighbors with our words is that our good will gets adulterated, in spite of ourselves, before it can pass our lips. Mr. Macey, for example, coming one evening expressly to let Silas know that recent events had given him the advantage of standing more favorably in the opinion of a man whose judgment was not formed lightly, opened the conversation by saying, as soon as he had seated himself and adjusted his thumbs:

"Come, Master Marner, why, you've no call to sit amoaning. You're a deal better off to ha' lost your money, nor to ha' kep' it by foul means. I used to think, when you first come into these parts, as you were no better nor you should be; you were younger a deal than what you are now; but you were allays a staring, white-faced creatur, partly like a bald-faced calf, as I may say. But there's no knowing; it isn't every queer-looked thing as Old Harry's had the making of—I mean, speaking o' toads and such; for they're often harmless and useful against varmin. And it's pretty much the same wi' you, as fur as I can see. Though as to the herbs and stuff to cure the breathing, if you brought that sort o' knowledge from distant parts, you might ha' been a bit freer of it. And if the knowledge wasn't well come by, why, you might ha' made up for it by coming to church reg'lar. And so, Master Marner, as I was saying—for there's windings i' things as they may carry you to the fur end o' the prayer book afore you get back to 'em—my advice is as you keep up your sperrits; for as for thinking you're a deep un and ha' got more inside you nor 'ull bear daylight, I'm not o' that opinion at all and so I tell the neighbors. For, says I, you talk o' Master Marner making out a tale—why it's nonsense, that is. It 'ud take a 'cute man to make a tale like that; and, says I, he looked as scared as a rabbit."

During this discursive address Silas had continued motionless in his previous attitude, leaning his elbows on his knees and pressing his hands against his head. Mr. Macey, not doubting that he had been listened to, paused, in the expectation of some appreciatory reply, but Marner remained silent. He had a sense that the old man meant to be good-natured and neighborly; but the kindness fell on him as sunshine falls on the wretched—he had no heart to taste it and felt that it was very far off him.

"Come, Master Marner, have you got nothing to say to that?" said Mr. Macey at last, with a slight accent of impatience.

"Oh," said Marner slowly, shaking his head between his hands, "I thank you—thank you kindly."

"Ay, ay, to be sure; I thought you would," said Mr. Macey; "and my advice is—have you got a Sunday suit?"

"No," said Marner.

"I doubted it was so," said Mr. Macey. "Now, let me advise you to get a Sunday suit. There's Tookey. He's a poor creatur—but he's got my tailoring business and some o' my money in it, and he shall make a suit at a low price, and give you trust. Then you can come to church and be a bit neighborly. Why, you've never heared me say 'Amen' since you come into these parts, and I recommend you to lose no time, for it'll be poor work when Tookey has it all to himself, for I mayn't be equil to stand i' the desk at all, come another winter." Here Mr. Macey paused, perhaps expecting some sign of emotion in his hearer, but not observing any, he went on. "And as for the money for the suit o' clothes, why, you get a matter of a pound a week at your weaving, Master Marner, and you're a young man, eh, for all you look so mushed. Why, you couldn't ha' been five and twenty when you come into these parts, eh?"

Silas started a little at the change to a questioning tone, and answered mildly, "I don't know; I can't rightly say. It's a long while since."

After receiving such an answer as this, it is not surprising that Mr. Macey observed later on in the evening at the Rainbow that Marner's head was "all of a muddle" and that it was to be doubted if he ever knew when Sunday came round, which showed him a worse heathen than many a dog.

Another of Silas's comforters, besides Mr. Macey, came to him with a mind highly charged on the same topic. This was Mrs. Winthrop, the wheelwright's wife. The inhabitants of Raveloe were not severely regular in their churchgoing, and perhaps there was hardly a person in the parish who would not have held that to go to church every Sunday in the calendar would have shown a greedy desire to stand well with Heaven and get an undue advantage over their neighbors. At the same time, it was understood to be requisite for all who were not household servants, or young men, to go to church at one of the great festivals; Squire Cass himself took it on Christmas Day; while those who were held to be "good livers" went to church with greater, though still with moderate, frequency.

Mrs. Winthrop was one of these. She was in all respects a woman of scrupulous conscience, so eager for duties that life seemed to offer them too scantily unless she rose at half-past four, though this threw a scarcity of work over the more advanced hours of the morning, which it was a constant problem with her to remove. Yet she had not the vixenish temper that is sometimes supposed to be a necessary condition of such habits. She was a very mild, patient woman, whose nature it was to seek out all the sadder and more serious elements of life, and pasture her mind upon them. She was the person always first thought of in Raveloe when there was illness or death in the family, when leeches were to be applied, or there was a sudden disappointment in a monthly nurse. She was a "comfortable woman"—good-looking, fresh-complexioned, having her lips always slightly screwed, as if she felt herself in a sickroom with a doctor or the clergyman present. She was never whimpering; no one had seen her shed tears. She was simply grave and inclined to shake her head and sigh, almost imperceptibly, like a funeral mourner who is not a relation. It seemed surprising that Ben Winthrop, who loved jokes, got along so well with Dolly; but she took her husband's jokes and joviality as patiently as everything else, considering that "men *would* be so," and viewing the stronger sex in the light of animals whom it had pleased Heaven to make naturally troublesome, like bulls and turkey cocks.

This good, wholesome woman could hardly fail to have her mind drawn strongly toward Silas Marner, now that he appeared in the light of a sufferer; and one Sunday afternoon she took her little boy Aaron with her and went to call on Silas, carrying in her hand some small lard cakes, flat, pastelike articles much esteemed in Raveloe. Aaron, an apple-cheeked youngster of seven, with a clean, starched frill that looked like a plate for the apples, needed all his adventurous curiosity to embolden him against the possibility that the big-eyed weaver might do him some bodily injury; and his dubiety was much increased when, on arriving at Stone Pit, they heard the mysterious sound of the loom.

"Ah, it is as I thought," said Mrs. Winthrop sadly.

They had to knock loudly before Silas heard them; but when he did come to the door he showed no impatience, as he would once have done, at a visit that had been unasked for and unexpected. Formerly, his heart had been as a locked casket with its treasure inside; but now the casket was empty, and the lock was broken. Left groping in darkness, with his prop utterly gone, Silas had inevitably a sense, though a dull and half-despairing one, that if any help came to him it must come from without; and there was a slight stirring of expectation at the sight of his fellow men, a faint consciousness of dependence on their good will. He opened the door wide to admit Dolly, but without otherwise returning her greeting than by moving the armchair a few inches as a sign that she was to sit down in it. Dolly, as soon as she was seated, removed the white cloth that covered her lard cakes, and said in her gravest way:

"I'd a baking yisterday, Master Marner, and the lard cakes turned out better nor common, and I'd ha' asked you to accept some, if you'd thought well. I don't eat such things myself, for a bit o' bread's what I like from one year's end to the other. But men's stomichs are made so comical. They want a change, they do. I know. God help 'em."

Dolly sighed gently as she held out the cakes to Silas, who thanked her kindly and looked very close at them, absently, being accustomed to look so at everything he took into his hand—eyed all the while by the wondering bright orbs of the small Aaron, who had made a wall of his mother's chair and was peeping from behind it.

"There's letters pricked on 'em," said Dolly. "I can't read 'em myself, and there's nobody, not Mr. Macey himself, rightly knows what they mean; but they've a good meaning, for they're the same as is on the pulpit cloth at church. What are they, Aaron, my dear?"

Aaron retreated completely behind his outwork.

"Oh, stop, that's naughty," said his mother mildly. "Well, whativer the letters are, they've a good meaning; and it's a stamp as has been in our house, Ben says, ever since he was a little un and his mother used to put it on the cakes, and I've allays put it on too; for if there's any good, we've need of it i' this world."

"It's I.H.S.," said Silas, at which proof of learning Aaron peeped round the chair again.

"Well, to be sure, you can read 'em off," said Dolly. "Ben's read 'em to me many and many a time, but they slip out o' my mind again. The more's the pity, for they're good letters, else they wouldn't be in the church; and so I prick 'em on all the loaves and all the cakes, though sometimes they won't hold, because o' the rising. As I said, if there's any good to be got, we've need of it i' this world—that we have. I hope they'll bring good to you, Master Marner, for it's wi' that will I brought you the cakes, and you see the letters have held better nor common."

Silas was as unable to interpret the letters as Dolly, but there was no possibility of misunderstanding the desire to give comfort that made itself heard in her quiet tones. He said, with more feeling than before— "Thank you—thank you kindly." He laid down the cakes and seated himself absently—drearily unconscious of any distinct benefit toward which the cakes and the letters, or even Dolly's kindness, could tend for him.

"Ah, if there's good anywhere, we've need of it," repeated Dolly, who did not lightly forsake a serviceable phrase. She looked at Silas pityingly as she went on. "Didn't you hear the church bells this morning, Master Marner? I doubt you knew it was Sunday. Living so lone here, you lose your count, I daresay; and then, when your loom makes a noise, you can't hear the bells, more partic'lar now the frost kills the sound."

"Yes, I did; I heard 'em," said Silas, to whom Sunday bells were a mere accident of the day and not part of its sacredness. There had been no bells in Lantern Yard.

"Dear heart!" said Dolly, pausing before she spoke again. "What a pity it is you should work of a Sunday and not clean yourself—if you *didn't* go to church. If you'd a roasting bit, it might be as you couldn't leave it, being a lone man. But there's the bakehus, if you could make up your mind to spend a twopence on the oven now and then—not every week in course—I shouldn't like to do that myself—you might carry your bit o' dinner there, for it's nothing but right to have a bit o' summat hot of a Sunday and not to make it as you can't know your dinner from Saturday. Now, upo' Christmas Day, this blessed Christmas as is ever coming, if you was to take your dinner to the bakehus, and go to church, and see the holly and the yew, and hear the anthim, and then take the sacramen', you'd be a deal the better, and you'd know which end you stood on, and you could put your trust i' Him as knows better nor we do, seein' you'd ha' done what it lies on us all to do."

Dolly's exhortation, which was an unusually long effort of speech for her, was uttered in the soothing, persuasive tone with which she would have tried to

94

prevail on a sick man to take his medicine or a basin of gruel for which he had no appetite. Silas had never before been closely urged on the point of his absence from church, which had only been thought of as a part of his general queerness; and he was too direct and simple to evade Dolly's appeal.

"Nay, nay," he said, "I know nothing o' church. I've never been to church."

"No!" said Dolly, in a low tone of wonderment. Then, bethinking herself of Silas's advent from an unknown country, she said, "Could it ha' been as they'd no church where you was born?"

"Oh, yes," said Silas meditatively, sitting in his usual posture of leaning on his knees and supporting his head. "There was churches—a many—it was a big town, but I knew nothing of 'em—I went to chapel."

Dolly was much puzzled at this new word, but she was rather afraid of inquiring further, lest "chapel" might mean some haunt of wickedness.

Now, little Aaron, having become used to the weaver's awful presence, had advanced to his mother's side, and Silas, seeming to notice him for the first time, tried to return Dolly's signs of good will by offering the lad a bit of lard cake. Aaron shrank back a little and rubbed his head against his mother's shoulder, but still thought the piece of cake worth the risk of putting his hand out for it.

"Oh, for shame, Aaron," said his mother, taking him on her lap. "Why, you don't want cake again yet awhile. He's wonderful hearty," she went on, with a little sigh. "That he is, God knows. He's my youngest, and we spoil him sadly, for either me or the father must allays hev him in our sight—that we must."

She stroked Aaron's brown head and thought it must do Master Marner good to see such a "pictur of a child." But Marner, on the other side of the hearth, saw the neat-featured, rosy face as a mere dim round with two dark spots in it.

"And he's got a voice like a bird—you wouldn't think," Dolly went on. "He can sing a Christmas carril as his father's taught him, and I take it for a token as he'll come to good, as he can learn the good tunes so quick. Come, Aaron. Stan' up and sing the carril to Master Marner. Come."

Aaron replied by rubbing his forehead against his mother's shoulder.

"Oh, that's naughty," said Dolly, gently. "Stan' up, when Mother tells you, and let me hold the cake till you've done."

Aaron was not indisposed to display his talents, even to an ogre, under protecting circumstances; and after a few more signs of coyness, consisting chiefly of rubbing the backs of his hands over his eyes and then peeping between them at Master Marner to see if he looked anxious for the "carril" he at length allowed his head to be duly adjusted and standing behind the table, which let him appear above it only as far as his broad frill, so that he looked like a cherubic head untroubled with a body, he began with a clear chirp, and in a melody that had the rhythm of an industrious hammer:

God rest you, merry gentlemen,
  Let nothing you dismay,
For Jesus Christ our Savior
  Was born on Christmas Day.

Dolly listened with a devout look, glancing at Marner in some confidence that this strain would help to allure him to church.

The Christmas carol, with its hammerlike rhythm, had fallen on his ears as strange music, quite unlike a hymn, and had none of the effect Dolly contemplated.

96

But he wanted to show her that he was grateful, and the only mode that occurred to him was to offer Aaron a bit more cake.

"Oh, no, thank you, Master Marner," said Dolly, holding down Aaron's willing hands. "We must be going home now. And so I wish you good-by, Master Marner; and if you ever feel anyways bad in your inside, as you can't fend for yourself, I'll come and clean up for you and get you a bit o' victual, willingly. I beg and pray of you to leave off weaving of a Sunday, for it's bad for soul and body. The money as comes i' that way 'ull be a bad bed to lie down on at the last, if it doesn't fly away, nobody knows where, like the white frost. You'll excuse me being that free with you, Master Marner, for I wish you well—I do. Make your bow, Aaron."

Silas said "Good-by, and thank you kindly," as he opened the door for Dolly, but he couldn't help feeling relieved when she was gone—relieved that he might weave again and moan at his ease. And so, notwithstanding the honest persuasions of Mr. Macey and Dolly Winthrop, Silas spent his Christmas Day in loneliness, eating his meat in sadness of heart, though the meat had come to him as a neighborly present. In the morning he looked out on the black frost that seemed to press cruelly on every blade of grass, while the half-icy red pool of the quarry shivered under the bitter wind. Toward evening the snow began to fall and curtained from him even that dreary outlook, shutting him close up with his narrow grief. He sat in his robbed home through the livelong evening, not caring to close his shutters or lock his door, pressing his head between his hands and moaning, till the cold grasped him and told him that his fire was gray.

Nobody in this world but himself knew that he was the same Silas Marner who had once loved his fellow with tender love and trusted in an unseen goodness. Even to himself that past experience had become dim.

In Raveloe village the bells rang merrily, and the church was fuller than all through the rest of the year, with red faces among the abundant dark green boughs— faces prepared for a longer service than usual by an odorous breakfast of toast and warm drink. Those green boughs, the hymn and anthem never heard but at Christmas brought a vague, exulting sense, for which the grown men could as little have found words as the children. Something great and mysterious had been done for them in Heaven above and in earth below, which they were appropriating by their presence. Then the red faces made their way through the black, biting frost to their own homes, feeling themselves free for the rest of the day to eat, drink, and be merry, and using that freedom without diffidence.

At Squire Cass's family party that day, nobody mentioned Dunstan. Nobody was sorry for his absence, or feared it would be too long. The doctor and his wife, Uncle and Aunt Kimble, were there, and the annual Christmas talk was carried through without any omissions, rising to the climax of Mr. Kimble's experience when he walked the London hospitals thirty years back, together with striking professional anecdotes then gathered.

The party on Christmas Day, being a strictly family party, was not the preeminently brilliant celebration of the season at Red House. It was the great party on New Year's Eve that made the glory of Squire Cass's hospitality. This was the occasion when all the society of Raveloe and Tarley, whether old acquaintances separated by long rutty distances, or cooled acquaintances separated by misunderstandings concerning runaway calves, or acquaintances founded on intermittent condescension, counted on meeting and on comporting themselves with mutual appropriateness. This was the occasion on which fair dames who came on pillions sent their bandboxes before them, supplied with more than their evening costume; for the feast was not to end with a single evening, like a paltry town entertainment where the whole supply of eatables is put on the table at once and bedding is scanty. Red House was provisioned as if for a siege; and as for the spare featherbeds ready to be laid on floors, they were as plentiful as might naturally be expected in a family that had killed its own geese for many generations.

Godfrey Cass was looking forward to this New Year's Eve with a foolish, reckless longing that made him half deaf to his importunate companion, Anxiety.

"Dunsey will be coming home soon; there will be a great blowup, and how will you bribe his spite to silence?" said Anxiety.

"Oh, he won't come home before New Year's Eve, perhaps," said Godfrey; "and I shall sit by Nancy then, and get a kind look from her in spite of herself."

"Money is wanted in another quarter," said Anxiety in a louder voice, "and how will you get it without selling your mother's diamond pin? And if you don't get it . . .?"

"Well, something may happen to make things easier. At any rate, there's one pleasure for me close at hand: Nancy is coming."

"Yes, and suppose your father should bring matters to a point that will oblige you to decline marrying her—and to give your reasons?"

"Hold your tongue and don't worry me. I can see Nancy's eyes, just as they will look at me, and feel her hand in mine already."

But Anxiety went on, though in noisy Christmas company; refusing to be utterly quieted even by much revelry.

Chapter 11

Some women, I grant, would not appear to advantage seated on a pillion, and attired in a drab joseph and a drab beaver bonnet with a crown resembling a small stewpan; for a garment suggesting a coachman's greatcoat, cut out under an exiguity of cloth that would only allow of miniature capes, is not well adapted to conceal deficiencies of contour, nor is drab a color that will throw sallow cheeks into lively contrast. It was all the greater triumph to Miss Nancy Lammeter's beauty that she looked thoroughly bewitching in that costume, as, seated on the pillion behind her tall, erect father, she held one arm around him and looked down, with open-eyed anxiety, at the treacherous snow-covered pools and puddles that sent up formidable splashings of mud under the stamp of Dobbin's foot. A painter would, perhaps, have preferred her in those moments when she was free from self-consciousness; but certainly the bloom on her cheeks was at its highest point of contrast with the surrounding drab when she arrived at the door of Red House and saw Mr. Godfrey Cass ready to lift her from the pillion. She wished her sister Priscilla had come up at the same time behind the servant, for then she would have contrived that Mr. Godfrey should have lifted off Priscilla first, and, in the meantime, she would have persuaded her father to go round to the horseblock instead of alighting at the doorsteps. It was very painful, when you had made it quite clear to a young man that you were determined not to marry him, however much he might wish it, that he would still continue to pay you marked attentions. Besides, why didn't he always show the same attentions, if he meant them sincerely, instead of being so strange as Mr. Godfrey Cass was, sometimes behaving as if he didn't want to speak to her and taking no notice of her for weeks and weeks, and then, all on a sudden, flirting again? Moreover, it was quite plain he had no real love for her, else he would not let people have *that* to say of him which they did say. Did he suppose that Miss Nancy Lammeter was to be won by any man, squire or no squire, who led a bad life? That was not what she had been used to see in her own father, who was the soberest and best man in that countryside, only a little hot and hasty now and then, if things were not done to the minute.

All these thoughts rushed through Miss Nancy's mind, in their habitual succession, in the moments between her first sight of Mr. Godfrey Cass standing at the door and her own arrival there. Happily, the Squire came out, too, and gave a loud greeting to her father so that, somehow, under cover of this noise she seemed to find concealment for her confusion and neglect of any suitably formal behavior while she was being lifted from the pillion by strong arms which seemed to find her ridiculously small and light. There was the best reason for hastening into the house at once since the snow was beginning to fall again, threatening an unpleasant journey for such guests as were still on the road. These were a small minority; for already the afternoon was beginning to decline, and there would not be too much time for the ladies who came from a distance to attire themselves in readiness for the early tea which was to inspirit them for the party.

There was a buzz of voices through the house, as Miss Nancy entered, mingled with the scrape of a fiddle preluding in the kitchen; but the Lammeters were guests whose arrival had evidently been thought of so much that it had been watched for from the windows, for Mrs. Kimble, who did the honors at Red House on these great occasions, came forward to meet Miss Nancy in the hall and conduct her upstairs. Mrs. Kimble was the Squire's sister, as well as the doctor's wife—a double dignity, with which her diameter was in direct proportion; so that, a journey upstairs being rather fatiguing to her, she did not oppose Miss Nancy's request to be allowed to find her way alone to the Blue Room where the Miss Lammeters' bandboxes had been deposited on their arrival in the morning.

There was hardly a bedroom in the house where feminine compliments were not passing and feminine toilettes going forward, in various stages, in space made scanty by extra beds spread upon the floor; and Miss Nancy, as she entered the Blue Room, had to make her little formal curtsy to a group of six. On the one hand, there were ladies no less important than the two Miss Gunns, the merchant's daughters from Lytherly, dressed in the height of fashion, with the tightest skirts and the shortest waists, and gazed at by Miss Ladbrook with a shyness not unsustained by inward criticism. Partly, Miss Ladbrook felt that her own skirt must be regarded as unduly lax by the Miss Gunns, and partly, that it was a pity the Miss Gunns did not show that judgment which she herself would show, if she were in their place, by stopping a little on this side of the fashion. On the other hand, Mrs. Ladbrook was standing in skullcap and front, with her turban in her hand, curtsying and smiling blandly and saying, "After you, ma'am," to another lady in similar circumstances, who had politely offered the precedence at the looking glass.

Miss Nancy had no sooner made her curtsy than an elderly lady came forward, whose full white muslin kerchief and mobcap round her curls of smooth gray hair were in daring contrast with the puffed yellow satins and topknotted caps of her neighbors. She approached Miss Nancy with much primness and said with a slow, treble suavity:

"Niece, I hope I see you well in health." Miss Nancy kissed her aunt's cheek dutifully and answered with the same sort of amiable primness, "Quite well, I thank you, Aunt. I hope I see you the same."

"Thank you, Niece; I keep my health for the present. And how is my brother-in-law?"

These dutiful questions and answers were continued until it was ascertained in detail that the Lammeters were all as well as usual and the Osgoods likewise; also that Niece Priscilla must certainly arrive shortly and that traveling on pillions in snowy weather was unpleasant, though a joseph was a great protection. Then Nancy was formally introduced to her aunt's visitors, the Miss Gunns, as being the daughters of a mother known to *their* mother, though now for the first time induced to make a journey into these parts. These ladies were so taken by surprise at finding such a lovely face and figure in an out-of-the-way country place that they began to feel some curiosity about the dress she would put on when she took off her joseph. Miss Nancy, whose thoughts were always conducted with the propriety and moderation conspicuous in her manners, remarked to herself that the Miss Gunns were rather hard-featured than otherwise and that such very low dresses as they wore might have been attributed to vanity if their shoulders had been pretty, but that, being as they were, it was not reasonable to suppose that they showed their necks from a love of display, but rather from some obligation not inconsistent with sense and modesty.

Three of the ladies quickly retired, but the Miss Gunns were quite content that Mrs. Osgood's inclination to remain with her niece gave them also a reason for staying to see the rustic beauty's toilette. It was really a pleasure—from the first opening of the bandbox, where everything smelt of lavender and rose

103

leaves, to the clasping of the small coral necklace that fitted closely round her little, white neck. Everything belonging to Miss Nancy was of delicate purity and nattiness; not a crease was where it had no business to be, not a bit of her linen professed whiteness without fulfilling its profession; the very pins on her pincushion were stuck in after a pattern from which she was careful to allow no aberration; and as for her own person, it gave the same idea of perfect, unvarying neatness as the body of a little bird. It is true that her light brown hair was cropped behind like a boy's, and was dressed in front in a number of flat rings that lay quite away from her face; but there was no sort of coiffure that could make Miss Nancy's cheeks and neck look otherwise than pretty; and when at last she stood complete in her silvery twilled silk, her lace tucker, her coral necklace, and coral eardrops, the Miss Gunns could see nothing to criticize except her hands, which bore the traces of buttermaking, cheese crushing, and even still coarser work. Miss Nancy was not ashamed of that, for while she was dressing she narrated to her aunt how she and Priscilla had packed their boxes yesterday because this morning was baking morning, and since they were leaving home, it was desirable to make a good supply of meat pies for the kitchen. As she concluded this judicious remark, she turned to the Miss Gunns that she might not commit the rudeness of not including them in the conversation. The Miss Gunns smiled stiffly and thought what a pity it was that these rich country people, who could afford to buy such good clothes (really Miss Nancy's lace and silk were very costly), should be brought up in utter ignorance and vulgarity. She actually said "mate" for "meat," "'appen" for "perhaps," and "'oss" for "horse," which to young ladies living in good Lytherly society, who habitually said "'orse," even in domestic privacy, and only said "'appen" on the right occasions, was necessarily shocking. Miss Nancy, indeed, had never been to any school higher than Dame Tedman's; and her acquaintance with literature hardly went beyond the rhymes she had worked in her large sampler. Yet she had the essential attributes of a lady—high veracity, delicate honor in her dealings, deference to others, and refined personal habits. Lest these should not suffice to convince grammatically fair ones that her feelings can at all resemble theirs, I will add that she was slightly proud and exacting, and as constant in her affection toward a baseless opinion as toward an erring beau.

The anxiety about sister Priscilla, which had grown rather active by the time the coral necklace was clasped, was happily ended by the entrance of that cheerful-looking lady herself, with a face made blowsy by cold and damp. After the first questions and greetings, she turned to Nancy and surveyed her from head to foot—then wheeled her round to ascertain that the back view was equally faultless.

"What do you think o' *these* gowns, Aunt Osgood?" said Priscilla, while Nancy helped her to unrobe.

"Very handsome indeed, Niece," said Mrs. Osgood, with a slight increase of formality. She always thought Niece Priscilla too rough.

"I'm obliged to have the same as Nancy, you know, for all I'm five years older, and it makes me look yellow; for she never *will* have anything without I have mine just like it because she wants us to look like sisters. And I tell her, folks 'ull think it's my weakness makes me fancy as I shall look pretty in what she looks pretty in. I *am* ugly—there's no denying that; I feature my father's family. But, law! I don't mind, do you?" Priscilla here turned to the Miss Gunns, rattling on in too much preoccupation with the delight of talking to notice that her candor was not appreciated.

"The pretty uns do for flycatchers—they keep the men away from us. I've no opinion o' the men, Miss Gunn. I don't know what *you* have. And as for fretting and stewing about what *they'll* think of you from morning till night, and making your life uneasy about what they're doing when they're out o' your sight—as I tell Nancy, it's a folly no woman need be guilty of, if she's got a good father and a good home. Let her leave it to them as have got no fortin and can't help themselves. As I say, Mr. Have-your-own-way is the best husband and the only one I'd ever promise to obey."

The delicate process of getting her narrow gown over her head without injury to her smooth curls obliged Miss Priscilla to pause in this rapid survey of life, and Mrs. Osgood seized the opportunity of rising and saying—

"Well, Niece, you'll follow us. The Miss Gunns will like to go down."

"Sister," said Nancy when they were alone, "you've offended the Miss Gunns, I'm sure."

"What have I done, child?" said Priscilla in some alarm.

"Why, you asked them if they minded about being ugly—you're so very blunt."

"Law, did I? Well, it popped out. It's a mercy I said no more, for I'm a bad un to live with folks when they don't like the truth. But as for being ugly, look at me, child, in this silver-colored silk. I told you how it 'ud be. I look as yellow as a daffadil. Anybody 'ud say you wanted to make a mawkin of me."

"No, Priscy, don't say so. I begged and prayed of you not to let us have this silk if you'd like another better. I was willing to have *your* choice. You know I was," said Nancy in anxious self-vindication.

"Nonsense, child! You know you'd set your heart on this; and reason good, for you're the color o' cream. It

106

'ud be fine doings for you to dress yourself to suit *my* skin. What I find fault with is that notion o' yours as I must dress myself just like you. But you do as you like with me—you always did from when first you begun to walk. Come, we can go down now. I'm as ready as a mawkin *can* be. There's nothing a-wanting to frighten the crows now I've got my eardroppers in."

As the two Miss Lammeters walked into the large parlor together, anyone who did not know the character of both might certainly have supposed that the reason why the square-shouldered, clumsy, high-featured Priscilla wore a dress the facsimile of her pretty sister's was either the mistaken vanity of the one or the malicious contrivance of the other in order to set off her own rare beauty. But the good-natured, self-forgetful cheeriness and common sense of Priscilla would soon have dissipated the one suspicion; and the modest calm of Nancy's speech and manners told clearly of a mind free from all disavowed devices.

Places of honor had been kept for the Miss Lammeters near the head of the principal tea table in the wainscoted parlor, now looking fresh and pleasant with handsome branches of holly, yew, and laurel from the abundant growths of the old garden; and Nancy felt an inward flutter, that no firmness of purpose could prevent, when she saw Mr. Godfrey Cass advancing to lead her to a seat between himself and Mr. Crackenthorp, while Priscilla was called to the opposite side between her father and the Squire. It certainly did make some difference to Nancy that the beau she had given up was the young man of quite the highest consequence in the parish—at home in a venerable and unique parlor, which was the extremity of grandeur in her experience, a parlor where *she* might one day have been mistress—and with the consciousness that she was spoken of as "Madame Cass," the Squire's wife. These circumstances exalted her inward drama in her own eyes and deepened the emphasis with which she declared to herself that not the most dazzling rank should induce her to marry a man whose conduct showed him careless of his character, but that "love once, love always," was the motto of a true and pure woman, and no man should ever have any right over her who would call on her to destroy the dried flowers that she treasured, and always would treasure, for Godfrey Cass's sake. Nancy was capable of keeping her word to herself under very trying conditions. Nothing but a becoming blush betrayed the moving thoughts that urged themselves upon her as she accepted the seat next to Mr. Crackenthorp; for she was so instinctively neat and adroit in all her actions, and her pretty lips met each other with such quiet firmness that it would have been difficult for her to appear agitated.

It was not the rector's practice to let a charming blush pass without an appropriate compliment. He was not in the least lofty or aristocratic, but simply a merry-eyed, small-featured, gray-haired man, with his chin propped by an ample, many-creased white neckcloth that seemed to predominate over every other point in his person and somehow impressed its peculiar character on his remarks.

"Ha, Miss Nancy," he said, turning his head within his cravat and smiling down pleasantly upon her, "when anybody pretends this has been a severe winter, I shall tell them I saw the roses blooming on New Year's Eve—ey, Godfrey. What do *you* say?"

Godfrey made no reply and avoided looking at Nancy very markedly; for though these complementary personalities were held to be in excellent taste in old-fashioned Raveloe society, reverent love has a politeness of its own that it teaches to men otherwise of small schooling. The Squire was rather impatient at Godfrey's showing himself a dull spark in this way. By this advanced hour of the day, the Squire was always in higher spirits than we have seen him in at the breakfast table and felt it quite pleasant to fulfill the hereditary duty of being noisily jovial and patronizing. At present, the Squire had only given an express welcome to the heads of families as they appeared; but always as the evening deepened, his hospitality rayed out more widely, till he had tapped the youngest guests on the back and shown a peculiar fondness for their presence, in the full belief that they must feel their lives made happy by their belonging to a parish where there was such a hearty man as Squire Cass to invite them and wish them well. Even in this early stage of the jovial mood, it was natural that he should wish to supply his son's deficiencies by looking and speaking for him.

"Ay, ay," he said to Mr. Lammeter, "us old fellows may wish ourselves young tonight when we see the mistletoe bough in the White Parlor. It's true, most things are gone back'ard in these last thirty years—the country's going down since the old king fell ill. But when I look at Miss Nancy here, I begin to think the lasses keep up their quality. No matter how hard I try, I can't remember a sample to match her, not even when I was a fine, young fellow and thought a deal about my pigtail. No offense to you, madam," he added, bending to Mrs. Crackenthorp, who sat by him, "I didn't know *you* when you were as young as Miss Nancy here."

Mrs. Crackenthorp—a small, blinking woman, who fidgeted incessantly with her lace, ribbons, and gold chain, turning her head about and making subdued noises very much like a guinea pig that twitches its nose and soliloquizes in all company indiscriminately— now blinked and fidgeted toward the Squire and said, "Oh, no—no offense."

This emphatic compliment of the Squire's to Nancy was felt by others, besides Godfrey, to have a diplomatic significance; and her father gave a slight additional erectness to his back as he looked across the table at her with complacent gravity. That grave and orderly senior was not going to bate a jot of his dignity by seeming elated at the notion of a match between his family and the Squire's. He was gratified by any honor paid to his daughter; but he must see an alteration in several ways before his consent would be vouchsafed. His spare but healthy person and high-featured, firm face, which looked as if it had never been flushed by excess, was in strong contrast, not only with the Squire's, but with the appearance of the Raveloe farmers generally—in accordance with a favorite saying of his own that "breed was stronger than pasture."

"Miss Nancy's wonderful like what her mother was, though, isn't she, Kimble?" said the stout lady of that name, looking round for her husband.

Doctor Kimble (country apothecaries in old days enjoyed that title without authority of diploma), being a thin and agile man, was flitting about the room with his hands in his pockets and making himself agreeable to his feminine patients with medical impartiality.

"Did you speak to me, my dear?" said the authentic doctor, coming quickly to his wife's side; but, as if foreseeing that she would be too much out of breath to repeat her remark, he went on immediately, "Ha, Miss Priscilla, the sight of you revives the taste of that superexcellent pork pie. I hope the batch isn't near an end."

"Yes, indeed, it is, Doctor," said Priscilla, "but I'll answer the next shall be as good. My pork pies don't turn out well by chance."

"Not as your doctoring does, eh, Kimble!—because folks forget to take your physic, eh?" said the Squire, who regarded physic and doctors as many loyal churchmen regard the church and the clergy—tasting a joke against them when he was in health, but impatiently eager for their aid when anything was the matter with him. He looked round with a triumphant laugh.

"Ah, she has a quick wit, my friend Priscilla has," said the doctor, choosing to attribute the epigram to a lady rather than allow a brother-in-law that advantage over him. "She saves a little pepper to sprinkle over her talk—that's the reason why she never puts too much into her pies. There's my wife, now, she never has an answer at her tongue's end. If I offend her, she's sure to scarify my throat with black pepper the next day, or else give me the colic with watery greens. That's an awful tit for tat." Here the vivacious doctor made a pathetic grimace.

"Did you ever hear the like?" said Mrs. Kimble, laughing above her double chin with much good humor, aside to Mrs. Crackenthorp, who blinked and nodded, and amiably intended to smile, but the intention lost itself in small twitchings and noises.

"I suppose that's the sort of tit for tat adopted in your profession, Kimble—if you've a grudge against a patient," said the rector.

"Never do have a grudge against our patients," said Mr. Kimble, "except when they leave us; and then, you see, we haven't the chance of prescribing for 'em. Ha, Miss Nancy," he continued, suddenly skipping to Nancy's side, "you won't forget your promise? You're to save a moment for me, you know."

"Come, come, Kimble, don't you be too for'ard," said the Squire. "Give the young uns fair play. There's my son Godfrey'll be wanting to have a round with you if you run off with Miss Nancy. He's bespoke her first, I'll be bound. Eh, sir! what do you say?" he continued, throwing himself backward and looking at Godfrey. "Haven't you asked Miss Nancy to sit with you?"

Godfrey, sorely uncomfortable under this significant insistence about Nancy, and afraid to think where it would end by the time his father had set his usual hospitable example of revelry before and after supper, saw no course open but to turn to Nancy and say, with as little awkwardness as possible—

"No, I've not asked her yet, but I hope she'll consent—if somebody else hasn't been before me."

"No, I've not engaged myself," said Nancy quietly, though blushingly. (If Mr. Godfrey founded any hopes on her consenting to sit with him, he would soon be undeceived; but there was no need for her to be uncivil.)

"Then I hope you've no objections to sitting with me," said Godfrey, beginning to lose the sense that there was anything uncomfortable in this arrangement.

"No, no objections," said Nancy, in a cold tone.

"Ah, well, you're a lucky fellow, Godfrey," said Uncle Kimble; "but you're my godson so I won't stand in your way. Else I'm not so very old, eh, my dear?" he went on, skipping to his wife's side again. "You wouldn't mind my having a second after you were gone—not if I cried a good deal first?"

"Come, come, take a cup o' tea and stop your tongue," said good-humored Mrs. Kimble, feeling some pride in a husband who must be regarded as so clever and amusing by the company generally. If he had only not been irritable!

While safe, well-tested personalities were enlivening the tea in this way, the sound of the fiddle, approaching within a distance at which it could be heard distinctly, made the young people look at each other with sympathetic impatience for the end of the meal.

"Why, there's Solomon in the hall," said the Squire, "and playing my fav'rite tune, *I* believe, 'The Flaxen-

Headed Ploughboy.' He's for giving us a hint as we aren't enough in a hurry to hear him play. Bob," he called out to his third long-legged son, who was at the other end of the room, "open the door, and tell Solomon to come in. He shall give us a tune here."

Bob obeyed, and Solomon walked in, fiddling as he walked, for he would on no account break off in the middle of a tune.

"Here, Solomon," said the Squire, with loud patronage. "Round here, my man. Ah, I knew it was 'The Flaxen-Headed Ploughboy.'"

Solomon Macey, a small, hale old man, with an abundant crop of long white hair, reaching nearly to his shoulders, advanced to the indicated spot, bowing reverently while he fiddled, as much as to say that he respected the company though he respected the keynote more. As soon as he had repeated the tune and lowered his fiddle, he bowed again to the Squire and the rector, and said, "I hope I see your honor and your reverence well and wishing you health and long life and a happy New Year. And wishing the same to you, Mr. Lammeter, sir; and to the other gentlemen, and the madams, and the young lasses."

As Solomon uttered the last words, he bowed in all directions solicitously, lest he should be wanting in due respect. But thereupon he immediately began to prelude and fell into the tune, which he knew would be taken as a special compliment by Mr. Lammeter.

"Thank ye, Solomon, thank ye," said Mr. Lammeter when the fiddle paused again. "That's 'Over the Hills and Far Away,' that is. My father used to say to me, whenever we heard that tune, 'Ah, lad, I come from over the hills and far away.' There's a many tunes I don't make head or tail of, but that speaks to me like the blackbird's whistle. I suppose it's the name; there's a deal in the name of a tune."

Solomon was already impatient to prelude again, and presently broke with much spirit into "Sir Roger de Coverley," at which there was a sound of chairs pushed back and laughing voices.

"Ay, ay, Solomon, we know what that means," said the Squire, rising. "It's time to begin the music, eh? Lead the way then, and we'll all follow you."

So Solomon, holding his white head on one side, and playing vigorously, marched forward at the head of the gay procession into the White Parlor, where the mistletoe bough was hung and multitudinous tallow candles made rather a brilliant effect, gleaming from among the berried holly boughs and reflected in the old-fashioned oval mirrors fastened in the panels of the white wainscot. A quaint procession! Old Solomon, in his seedy clothes and long white locks, seemed to be luring that decent company by the magic scream of his fiddle—luring discreet matrons in turban-shaped caps, nay, Mrs. Crackenthorp herself, the summit of whose perpendicular feather was on a level with the Squire's shoulder—luring fair lasses complacently conscious of very short waists and skirts blameless of front folds—luring burly fathers in large variegated waistcoats, and luring ruddy sons, for the most part shy and sheepish, in short nether garments and very long coattails.

Already Mr. Macey and a few other privileged villagers, who were allowed to be spectators on these great occasions, were seated on benches placed for them near the door. Great was the admiration and satisfaction in that quarter when the couples had seated themselves. "Look at Mrs. Osgood," said Ben Winthrop, who was holding his son Aaron between his knees. She doesn't look a day older nor last year."

"Fayder," said Aaron, whose feet were busy beating out the tune, "how does that big cock's feather stick in

114

Mrs. Crackenthorp's head? Is there a little hole for it, like in my shuttlecock?"

"Hush, lad, hush; that's the way the ladies dress theirselves, that is," said the father, adding, however, in an undertone to Mr. Macey, "It does make her look funny, though—partly like a short-necked bottle wi' a long quill in it. Hey, by jingo, there's the young Squire wi' Miss Nancy! There's a lass for you—like a pink-and-white posy! There's nobody 'ud think as anybody could be so pritty. I shouldn't wonder if she's Madam Cass some day, after all—and nobody is more rightfuller, for they'd make a fine match. You can find nothing against Master Godfrey's shapes, Macey, I'll bet a penny."

Mr. Macey screwed up his mouth, leaned his head further on one side, and twirled his thumbs with a presto movement as his eyes followed Godfrey. At last he summed up his opinion.

"Pretty well down'ard, but a bit too round i' the shoulder blades. As for them coats as he gets from the Flitton tailor, they're a poor cut to pay double money for."

"Ah, Mr. Macey, you and me are two folks," said Ben, slightly indignant at this carping. "I should like you to pick me out a finer-limbed young fellow nor Master Godfrey—one as 'ud knock you down easier, or 's more pleasanter looksed when he's piert and merry."

"Tchuh!" said Mr. Macey, provoked to increased severity, "He isn't come to his right color yet; he's partly like a slack-baked pie. I wouldn't doubt he's got a soft place in his head, else why should he be turned round the finger by that offal Dunsey, as nobody's seen o' late, and let him kill that fine hunting hoss as was the talk o' the country? For a while he was allays after Miss Nancy, and then it all went off again, like a smell o' hot porridge, as I may say. That wasn't my way when I went a-courting."

115

"Ay, but mayhap Miss Nancy hung off like, and your lass didn't," said Ben.

"I should say she didn't," said Mr. Macey significantly. "Before I said 'sniff,' I took care to know as she'd say 'snaff,' and pretty quick too. I wasn't a-going to open *my* mouth, like a dog at a fly, and snap it to again wi' nothing to swaller."

"Well, I think Miss Nancy's a-coming round again," said Ben, "for Master Godfrey doesn't look so downhearted tonight. And I see he's for taking her away to sit down. That looks like sweethearting, that does."

The reason why Godfrey and Nancy had left the party was not so tender as Ben imagined. In the close press of couples, a slight accident had happened to Nancy's dress, which, while it was short enough to show her neat ankle in front, was long enough behind to be caught under the stately stamp of the Squire's foot, so as to rend certain stitches at the waist and cause much sisterly agitation in Priscilla's mind, as well as serious concern in Nancy's. One's thoughts may be much occupied with love struggles, but hardly so as to be insensible to a disorder in the general framework of things. Nancy said to Godfrey, with a deep blush, that she must go and sit down till Priscilla could come to her; for the sisters had already exchanged a short whisper and an open-eyed glance full of meaning. No reason less urgent than this could have prevailed on Nancy to give Godfrey this opportunity of sitting apart with her. As for Godfrey, he was feeling so happy and oblivious under the long charm of Nancy that he got rather bold on the strength of her confusion and was capable of leading her straight away, without leave asked, into the adjoining small parlor.

"Oh, no, thank you," said Nancy, coldly, as soon as she perceived where he was going, "not in there. I'll wait here till Priscilla's ready to come to me. I'm sorry to bring you out and make myself troublesome."

"Why, you'll be more comfortable here by yourself," said the artful Godfrey; "I'll leave you here till your sister can come." He spoke in an indifferent tone.

That was an agreeable proposition, and just what Nancy desired; why then, was she a little hurt that Mr. Godfrey should make it? They entered, and she seated herself on a chair against one of the tables, as the stiffest and most unapproachable position she could choose.

"Thank you, sir," she said immediately. "I needn't give you any more trouble."

"That's very ill-natured of you," said Godfrey, standing by her without any sign of intended departure.

"Oh, no, sir, I don't mean to say what's ill-natured at

all," said Nancy, looking distractingly prim and pretty. "When gentlemen have so many pleasures, one moment can matter but very little."

"You know that isn't true. You know one moment with you matters more to me than all the other pleasures in the world."

It was a long, long while since Godfrey had said anything so direct as that, and Nancy was startled. Her instinctive dignity and repugnance to any show of emotion made her sit perfectly still and only throw a little more decision into her voice, as she said:

"No, indeed, Mr. Godfrey, that's not known to me, and I have very good reasons for thinking different. But if it's true, I don't wish to hear it."

"Would you never forgive me, then, Nancy—never think well of me, let what would happen? Would you never think the present made amends for the past? Not if I turned a good fellow and gave up everything you didn't like?"

Godfrey was half conscious that this sudden opportunity of speaking to Nancy alone had driven him beside himself; but blind feeling had got the mastery of his tongue. Nancy really felt much agitated by the possibility Godfrey's words suggested, but this very pressure of emotion that she was in danger of finding too strong for her roused all her power of self-command.

"I should be glad to see a good change in anybody, Mr. Godfrey," she answered, with the slightest discernible difference of tone, "but it 'ud be better if no change was wanted."

"You're very hardhearted, Nancy," said Godfrey pettishly. "You might encourage me to be a better fellow. I'm very miserable—but you've no feeling."

"I think those have the least feeling that act wrong to begin with," said Nancy, sending out a flash in spite of herself. Godfrey was delighted with that little flash and would have liked to go on and make her quarrel with him; Nancy was so exasperatingly quiet and firm, but she was not indifferent to him *yet*.

The entrance of Priscilla, bustling forward and saying, "Dear heart alive, child, let us look at this gown," cut off Godfrey's hopes of a quarrel.

"I suppose I must go now," he said to Priscilla.

"It's no matter to me whether you go or stay," said that frank lady, searching for something in her pocket, with a preoccupied brow.

"Do *you* want me to go?" said Godfrey, looking at Nancy, who was now standing up by Priscilla's order.

"As you like," said Nancy, trying to recover all her former coldness, and looking down carefully at the hem of her gown.

"Then I like to stay," said Godfrey, with a reckless determination to get as much of this joy as he could tonight and think nothing of the morrow.

Chapter 12

While Godfrey Cass was taking draughts of forgetfulness from the sweet presence of Nancy, willingly losing all sense of that hidden bond that at other moments galled and fretted him so as to mingle irritation with the very sunshine, Godfrey's wife was walking with slow, uncertain steps through the snow-covered Raveloe lanes, carrying her child in her arms.

This journey on New Year's Eve was a premeditated act of vengeance, which she had kept in her heart ever since Godfrey, in a fit of passion, had told her he would sooner die than acknowledge her as his wife. There would be a great party at Red House on New Year's Eve, she knew; her husband would be smiling and smiled upon, hiding *her* existence in the darkest corner of his heart. But she would mar his pleasure; she would go in her dingy rags, with her faded face, once as handsome as the best, with her little child that had its father's hair and eyes, and disclose herself to the Squire as his eldest son's wife. It is seldom that the miserable can help regarding their misery as a wrong inflicted by those who are less miserable. Molly knew the cause of her dingy rags was not her husband's neglect, but the demon Opium to whom she was enslaved, body and soul, except in the lingering mother's tenderness that refused to give him her hungry child. She knew this well; and yet, in the moments of wretched, unbenumbed consciousness, the sense of her want and degradation transformed itself continually into bitterness toward Godfrey. *He* was well-off, and if she had her rights, she would be well-off too. The belief that he repented his marriage and suffered from it only aggravated her vindictiveness.

She had set out at an early hour, but had lingered on the road, inclined by her indolence to believe that if she waited under a warm shed the snow would cease to fall. She had waited longer than she knew, and now that she found herself belated in the snow-hidden ruggedness of the long lanes, even the animation of a vindictive purpose could not keep her spirit from failing. It was seven o'clock, and by this time she was not very far from Raveloe, but she was not familiar enough with those monotonous lanes to know how near she was to her journey's end. She needed comfort, and she knew but one comforter—the familiar demon in her bosom. She hesitated a moment, after drawing out the black remnant, before she raised it to her lips. In that moment the mother's love pleaded for painful consciousness rather than oblivion—pleaded to be left in aching weariness rather than to have the encircling arms benumbed so that they could not feel the dear burden. In another moment Molly had flung something away, but it was not the black remnant—it was an empty vial. She walked on again under the breaking cloud, from which there came now and then the light of a quickly veiled star, for a freezing wind had sprung up since the snowing had ceased, but she walked always more and more drowsily and clutched more and more automatically the sleeping child at her bosom.

Slowly the demon was working his will, and cold and weariness were his helpers. Soon she felt nothing but a supreme immediate longing that curtained off all futurity—the longing to lie down and sleep. She had arrived at a spot where her footsteps were no longer checked by a hedgerow, and she had wandered vaguely, unable to distinguish any objects, notwithstanding the wide whiteness around her and the growing starlight. She sank down against a straggling furze bush, an easy pillow enough; and the bed of snow, too, was soft. She did not feel that the bed was cold, and did not heed whether the child would wake and cry for her. But her arms had not yet relaxed their instinctive clutch; and the little one slumbered on as gently as if it had been rocked in a lace-trimmed cradle.

The complete torpor came at last; the fingers lost their tension, the arms unbent; then the little head fell away from the bosom, and the blue eyes opened wide on the cold starlight. At first there was a little peevish cry of "Mammy!" and an effort to regain the pillowing arm and bosom; but mammy's ear was deaf, and the pillow seemed to be slipping away backward. Suddenly, as the child rolled downward on its mother's knees, all wet with snow, its eyes were caught by a bright glancing light on the white ground, and, with the ready transition of infancy, it was immediately absorbed in watching the bright, living thing running toward it, yet never arriving. That bright, living thing must be caught;

and in an instant the child had slipped on all fours and held out one little hand to catch the gleam. The gleam would not be caught in that way, and now the head was held up to see where the cunning gleam came from.

It came from a very bright place; and the little one, rising on its legs, toddled through the snow, the old, grimy shawl in which it was wrapped trailing behind it, and the queer little bonnet dangling at its back. It toddled on to the open door of Silas Marner's cottage and right up to the warm hearth, where there was a bright fire of logs and sticks that had thoroughly warmed the old sack (Silas's greatcoat) spread out on the bricks to dry. The little one, accustomed to be left to itself for long hours without notice from its mother, squatted down on the sack and spread its tiny hands toward the blaze in perfect contentment, gurgling and making many inarticulate communications to the cheerful fire, like a new-hatched gosling beginning to find itself comfortable. Presently the warmth had a lulling effect, and the little golden head sank down on the old sack, and the blue eyes were veiled by their delicate, half-transparent lids.

Where was Silas Marner while this strange visitor had come to his hearth? He was in the cottage, but he did not see the child. During the last few weeks since he had lost his money, he had contracted the habit of opening his door and looking out from time to time, as if he thought that his money might be somehow coming back to him or that some trace, some news of it, might be mysteriously on the road and be caught by the listening ear or the straining eye. It was chiefly at night, when he was not occupied in his loom, that he fell into this repetition of an act for which he could have assigned no definite purpose and which can hardly be understood except by those who have undergone a bewildering separation from a supremely loved object. In the evening twilight, and later whenever the night was not dark, Silas looked out on that narrow prospect round Stone Pit, listening and gazing, not with hope, but with mere yearning and unrest.

This morning he had been told by some of his neighbors that it was New Year's Eve and that he must sit up and hear the old year rung out and the new rung in, because that was good luck and might bring his money back again. This was only a friendly Raveloe way of jesting with the half-crazy oddities of a miser, but it had perhaps helped to throw Silas into a more than usually excited state. Since the oncoming of twilight, he had opened his door again and again, though only to shut it immediately at seeing all distance veiled by the falling snow. The last time he opened it, the snow had ceased and the clouds were parting here and there. He stood and listened and gazed for a long while. There was really something on the road coming toward him then, but he caught no sign of it. The stillness and the wide, trackless snow seemed to narrow his solitude and touched his yearning with the chill of despair. He went in again and put his right hand on the latch of the door to close it—but he did not close it. He was arrested, as he had been already since his loss, by the invisible wand of catalepsy, and he stood like a graven image with wide, but sightless eyes, holding open his door, powerless to resist either the good or evil that might enter there.

When Marner's sensibility returned, he continued the action that had been arrested and closed his door, unaware of the chasm in his consciousness, unaware of any intermediate change, except that the light had grown dim and that he was chilled and faint. He thought he had been too long standing at the door and looking out. Turning toward the hearth, where the two logs had fallen apart and sent forth only a red uncertain glimmer, he seated himself on his fireside chair and was stooping to push his logs together, when, to his blurred vision, it seemed as if there were gold on the floor in front of the hearth. Gold!—his own gold—brought back to him as mysteriously as it had been taken away! He felt his heart begin to beat violently, and for a few moments he was unable to stretch out his hand and grasp the restored treasure. The heap of gold seemed to glow and get larger beneath his agitated gaze. He leaned forward at last and stretched forth his hand; but instead of the hard coin with the familiar resisting outline, his fingers encountered soft, warm curls. In utter amazement, Silas fell on his knees and bent his head low to examine the marvel. It was a sleeping child—a round, fair thing, with soft, yellow rings all over its head. Could this be his little sister come back to him in a dream—his little sister whom he had carried about in his arms for a year before she died, when he was a small boy without shoes or stockings? That was the first thought that darted across Silas's blank wonderment. *Was* it a dream? He rose to his feet again, pushed his logs together, and, throwing on some dried leaves and sticks, raised a flame; but the flame did not disperse the vision. It only lit up more distinctly the little, round form of the child and its shabby clothing. It was very much like his little sister. Silas sank into his chair, powerless under the double presence of an inexplicable surprise and a hurrying influx of memories. How and when had the child come in without his knowledge? He had never been beyond the door. But along with that question, and almost thrusting it away, there was a vision of the old home and the old streets leading to Lantern Yard—and within that vision there was another, of the thoughts that had been present with him in those far-off scenes. The thoughts were strange to him now, like old friendships impossible to revive. Yet he had a dreamy feeling that this child was somehow a message come to him from that far-off life. It stirred fibers that had never been moved in Raveloe—old quiverings of tenderness—old impressions of awe at the presentiment of some Power presiding over his life. His imagination could not extricate itself from the sense of mystery in the child's sudden presence, and he had formed no conjectures of ordinary, natural means by which the event could have been brought about.

There was a cry on the hearth. The child had awaked, and Marner stooped to lift it on his knee. It clung round his neck and burst louder and louder into that mingling of inarticulate cries with "Mammy!" by which little children express the bewilderment of waking. Silas pressed it to him and almost unconsciously uttered sounds of hushing tenderness while he bethought himself that some of his porridge, which had got cool by the dying fire, would do to feed the child with, if it were only warmed up a little.

He had plenty to do through the next hour. The porridge, sweetened with some dry brown sugar from an old store that he had refrained from using for himself, stopped the cries of the little one and made her lift her blue eyes with a wide, quiet gaze at Silas as he put the spoon into her mouth. Presently, she slipped from his knee and began to toddle about, but with a pretty stagger that made Silas jump up and follow her lest she should fall against anything that would hurt her. She only fell in a sitting posture on the ground and began to pull at her boots, looking up at him with a crying face as if the boots hurt her. He took her on his knee again, but it was some time before it occurred to Silas's dull bachelor mind that the wet boots were the grievance, pressing on her warm ankles. He got them off with difficulty, and Baby was at once happily occupied with the primary mystery of her own toes, inviting Silas, with much chuckling, to consider the mystery too. The wet boots had at last suggested to Silas that the child had been walking on the snow, and this roused him from his entire oblivion of any ordinary means by which it could have entered or been brought into his house. Under the prompting of his new idea, and without waiting to form conjectures, he raised the child in his arms and went to the door. As soon as he had opened it, there was the cry of "Mammy!" again, which Silas had not heard since the child's first hungry waking. Bending forward, he could just discern the marks made by the little feet on the virgin snow, and he followed their track to the furze bushes. "Mammy!" the little one cried again and again, stretching itself forward so as almost to escape from Silas's arms, before he himself was aware that there was something more than the bush before him—that there was a human body, with the head sunk low in the furze, and half covered with the shaken snow.

Chapter 13

It was after the early suppertime at Red House, and the entertainment was in that stage when bashfulness itself had passed into easy jollity, when gentlemen, conscious of unusual accomplishments, could at length be prevailed on to play a hornpipe, and when the Squire preferred talking loudly and patting his visitors' backs. When the evening had advanced to this pitch of freedom and enjoyment, it was usual for the servants, the heavy duties of supper being well over, to get their share of amusement by coming to look on; so, the back regions of the house were left in solitude.

There were two doors by which the White Parlor was entered from the hall, and they were both standing open for the sake of air. The lower one was crowded with the servants and villagers, and only the upper doorway was left free. Godfrey was standing a little way off to keep sight of Nancy, who was seated in the group near her father. He stood aloof because he wished to avoid suggesting himself as a subject for the Squire's fatherly jokes in connection with matrimony and Miss Nancy Lammeter's beauty, which were likely to become more and more explicit. He had the prospect of speaking with her again when the music was concluded, and in the meanwhile, it was very pleasant to get long glances at her quite unobserved.

When Godfrey was lifting his eyes from one of those long glances, they encountered an object as startling to him at that moment as if it had been an apparition from the dead. It *was* an apparition from that hidden life which lies, like a dark bystreet, behind the goodly ornamented facade that meets the sunlight and the gaze of respectable admirers. It was his own child carried in Silas Marner's arms. That was his instantaneous impression, unaccompanied by doubt, though he had not seen the child for months past. When the hope was rising that he might possibly be mistaken, Mr. Crackenthorp and Mr. Lammeter had already advanced to Silas, in astonishment at this strange advent. Godfrey joined them immediately, unable to rest without hearing every word—trying to control himself, but conscious that if anyone noticed him, they must see that he was white-lipped and trembling.

Now, all eyes at that end of the room were bent on Silas Marner; the Squire himself had risen and asked angrily, "How's this? What's this? What do you do coming in here this way?"

"I'm come for the doctor—I want the doctor," Silas had said in the first moment to Mr. Crackenthorp.

"Why, what's the matter, Marner?" said the rector. "The doctor's here; but say quietly what you want him for."

"It's a woman," said Silas, speaking low, and half breathlessly just as Godfrey came up. "She's dead, I think—dead in the snow at the stone pit—not far from my door."

Godfrey felt a great throb. There was one terror in his mind at that moment. It was that the woman might *not* be dead. That was an evil terror—an ugly inmate to have found a nestling place in Godfrey's kindly disposition; but no disposition is a security from evil wishes to a man whose happiness hangs on duplicity.

"Hush, hush!" said Mr. Crackenthorp. "Go out into the hall there. I'll fetch the doctor to you. He's found a woman in the snow—and thinks she's dead," he added, speaking low to the Squire. "Better say as little about it as possible. It will shock the ladies. Just tell them a poor woman is ill from cold and hunger. I'll go and fetch Kimble."

By this time, however, the ladies had pressed forward, curious to know what could have brought the solitary linen weaver there under such strange circumstances, and interested in the pretty child, who, half alarmed and half attracted by the brightness and the numerous company, now frowned and hid her face, now lifted up her head again and looked round placably until a touch or a coaxing word brought back the frown and made her bury her face with new determination.

"What child is it?" said several ladies at once, and, among the rest, Nancy Lammeter, addressing Godfrey.

"I don't know—some poor woman's who has been found in the snow, I believe," was the answer Godfrey wrung from himself with a terrible effort. ("After all, *am* I certain?" he hastened to add, in anticipation of his own conscience.)

"Why, you'd better leave the child here, then, Master Marner," said good-natured Mrs. Kimble, hesitating, however, to take those dingy clothes into contact with her own ornamented satin bodice. "I'll tell one o' the girls to fetch it."

"No—no—I can't part with it, I can't let it go," said Silas abruptly. "It's come to me—I've a right to keep it."

The proposition to take the child from him had come to Silas quite unexpectedly, and his speech, uttered under a strong, sudden impulse, was almost like a revelation to himself. A minute before, he had no distinct intention about the child.

"Did you ever hear the like?" said Mrs. Kimble, in mild surprise, to her neighbor.

"Now, ladies, I must trouble you to stand aside," said Mr. Kimble, coming from the other room, in some bitterness at the interruption, but drilled by the long habit of his profession into obedience to unpleasant calls, even when he was hardly sober.

"It's nasty business turning out now, eh, Kimble?" said the Squire. "He might ha' gone for your young fellow—the 'prentice there—what's his name?"

"Might? Ay—what's the use of talking about might?" growled Uncle Kimble, hastening out with Marner and followed by Mr. Crackenthorp and Godfrey. "Get me a pair of thick boots, Godfrey, will you? And stay, let somebody run to Winthrop's and fetch Dolly—she's the best woman to get. Ben was here himself before supper. Is he gone?"

"Yes, sir, I met him," said Marner, "but I couldn't stop to tell him anything, only I said I was going for the doctor, and he said the doctor was at the Squire's. I made haste and ran, and there was nobody to be seen at the back o' the house, so I went in to where the company was."

The child, no longer distracted by the bright light and the smiling women's faces, began to cry and call for "Mammy!" though always clinging to Marner, who had apparently won her thorough confidence. Godfrey had come back with the boots, and felt the cry as if some fiber were drawn tight within him.

"I'll go," he said hastily, eager for some movement. "I'll go and fetch the woman—Mrs. Winthrop."

"Oh, pooh—send somebody else," said Uncle Kimble, hurrying away with Marner.

"You'll let me know if I can be of any use, Kimble," said Mr. Crackenthorp. But the doctor was out of hearing.

Godfrey, too, had disappeared. He was gone to snatch his hat and coat, having just reflection enough to remember that he must not look like a madman. He rushed out of the house into the snow without heeding his thin shoes.

In a few minutes he was on his rapid way to Stone Pit with Dolly, who, though feeling that she was entirely in her place in encountering cold and snow on an errand of mercy, was much concerned at a young gentleman's getting his feet wet under a like impulse.

"You'd a deal better go back, sir," said Dolly, with respectful compassion. "You've no call to catch cold; and I'd ask you if you'd be so good as to tell my husband to come—on your way back. He's at the Rainbow. Or else, there's Mrs. Snell 'ud happen send the boy up to fetch and carry, for there may be things wanted from the doctor's."

"No, I'll stay, now I'm once out. I'll stay outside here," said Godfrey when they came opposite Marner's cottage. "You can come and tell me if I can do anything."

"Well, sir, you're very good. You've a tender heart," said Dolly, going to the door.

Godfrey was too painfully preoccupied to feel a twinge of self-reproach at this undeserved praise. He walked up and down, unconscious that he was plunging ankle-deep in snow, unconscious of everything but trembling suspense about what was going on in the cottage and the effect of each alternative on his future lot. No, not quite unconscious of everything else, deeper down, and half smothered by passionate desire and dread, there was the sense that he ought not to be waiting on these alternatives; that he ought to accept the consequences of his deeds, own the miserable wife, and fulfill the claims of the helpless child. But he had not moral courage enough to contemplate that active renunciation of Nancy as possible for him. He had only conscience and heart enough to make him forever uneasy under the weakness that forbade the renunciation. At this moment, his mind leaped away from all restraint toward the sudden prospect of deliverance from his long bondage.

"Is she dead?" said the voice that predominated over every other within him. "If she is, I may marry Nancy; and then I shall be a good fellow in the future and have no secrets, and the child shall be taken care of

132

somehow." But across that vision came the other possibility—"She may live, and then it's all up with me."

Godfrey never knew how long it was before the door of the cottage opened and Mr. Kimble came out. He went forward to meet his uncle, prepared to suppress the agitation he must feel, whatever news he was to hear.

"I waited for you, as I'd come so far," he said, speaking first.

"Pooh, it was nonsense for you to come out. Why didn't you send one of the men? There's nothing to be done. She's dead—has been dead for hours, I should say."

"What sort of woman is she?" said Godfrey, feeling the blood rush to his face.

"A young woman, but emaciated, with long, black hair. Some vagrant—quite in rags. She's got a wedding ring on, however. They must fetch her away to the workhouse tomorrow. Come, come along."

"I want to look at her," said Godfrey. "I think I saw such a woman yesterday. I'll overtake you in a minute or two."

Mr. Kimble went on, and Godfrey turned back to the cottage. He cast only one glance at the dead face on the pillow, which Dolly had smoothed with decent care. He remembered that last look at his unhappy, hated wife so well that later at the end of sixteen years, every line in the worn face was present to him when he told the full story of this night.

He turned immediately toward the hearth, where Silas Marner sat lulling the child. She was perfectly quiet now, but not asleep—only soothed by sweet porridge and warmth into that wide-gazing calm that makes us older human beings, with our inward turmoil, feel a certain awe in the presence of a little child; such we feel before some quiet majesty or beauty in the earth or sky—before a steady glowing planet or a full-flowered eglantine, or the bending trees over a silent pathway. The wide-open blue eyes looked up at Godfrey's, without any uneasiness or sign of recognition. The child could make no visible, audible claim on its father, and the father felt a strange mixture of feelings, a conflict of regret and joy that the pulse of that little heart had no response for the half-jealous yearning in his own. When the blue eyes turned away from him slowly, they fixed themselves on the weaver's queer face, which was bent low down to look at them, while the small hand began to pull Marner's withered cheek with loving disfiguration.

"You'll take the child to the parish tomorrow?" asked Godfrey, speaking as indifferently as he could.

"Who says so?" said Marner sharply. "Will they make me take her?"

"Why, you wouldn't like to keep her, should you—an old bachelor like you?"

"I'll keep her till anybody shows they've a right to take her away from me," said Marner. "The mother's dead, and I reckon it's got no father; it's a lone thing—and I'm a lone thing. My money's gone, I don't know where—and this is come from I don't know where. I know nothing—I'm partly amazed."

"Poor little thing!" said Godfrey. "Let me give something toward finding it clothes."

He had put his hand in his pocket and found half a guinea, and, thrusting it into Silas's hand, he hurried out of the cottage to overtake Mr. Kimble.

"Ah, I see it's not the same woman I saw," he said, as he came up. "It's a pretty little child, and the old fellow seems to want to keep it. That's strange for a miser like him. I gave him a trifle to help him out. The parish isn't likely to quarrel with him for the right to keep the child."

"No, but I've seen the time when I might have quarreled with him for it myself. It's too late now, though. If the child ran into the fire, your aunt's too fat to overtake it; she could only sit and grunt like an alarmed sow. But what a fool you are, Godfrey, to come out in your evening shoes and stockings in this way—and you one of the beaux of the evening, and at your own house! What do you mean by such freaks, young fellow? Has Miss Nancy been cruel, and do you want to spite her by spoiling your pumps?"

"Oh, everything has been disagreeable tonight. I was tired to death of jigging and gallanting, and I'd had to speak with the other Miss Gunn," said Godfrey, glad of the subterfuge his uncle had suggested to him.

Godfrey reappeared in the White Parlor with dry feet, and, since the truth must be told, with a sense of relief and gladness that was too strong for painful thoughts to struggle with. Could he not venture now, whenever opportunity offered, to say the tenderest things to Nancy Lammeter—to promise her and himself that he would always be just what she would desire to see him? There was no danger that his dead wife would be recognized; those were not days of active inquiry and wide report; and as for the registry of their marriage, that was a long way off, buried in unturned pages, away from everyone's interest but his own. Dunsey might betray him if he came back, but Dunsey might be won to silence.

When events turn out so much better for a man than he has had reason to hope, is it not a proof that his conduct has been less foolish and blameworthy than it might otherwise have appeared? When we are treated well, we naturally begin to think that we are not altogether unmeritorious and that it is only just we should treat ourselves well and not mar our own good fortune. What, after all, would be the use of his confessing the past to Nancy Lammeter and throwing away his happiness?—nay, hers? For he felt some confidence that she loved him. As for the child, he would see that it was cared for; he would never forsake it; he would do everything but own it. Perhaps it would be just as happy in life without being owned by its father, seeing that nobody could tell how things would turn out, and that—is there any other reason wanted?—the father would be much happier without owning the child.

Chapter 14

There was a pauper's burial that week in Raveloe, and up Kench Yard at Batherley it was known that the dark-haired woman with the fair child, who had lately come to lodge there, was gone away again. That was all the express note taken that Molly had disappeared from the eyes of men. The unwept death which, to the general lot, seemed as trivial as the summer-shed leaf, was charged with the force of destiny to certain human lives that we know of, shaping their joys and sorrows even to the end.

Silas Marner's determination to keep the "tramp's child" was a matter of hardly less surprise and iterated talk in the village than the robbery of his money. That softening of feeling toward him that dated from his misfortune, that merging of suspicion and dislike in a rather contemptuous pity for him as lone and crazy, was now accompanied with a more active sympathy, especially amongst the women. Notable mothers, who knew what it was to keep children "whole and sweet," lazy mothers, who knew what it was to be interrupted in folding their arms and scratching their elbows by the mischievous propensities of a toddling child, were equally interested in conjecturing how a lone man would manage with a two-year-old child on his hands, and were equally ready with their suggestions. The notable chiefly telling him what he had better do, and the lazy ones being emphatic in telling him what he would never be able to do.

Among the notable mothers, Dolly Winthrop was the one whose neighborly offices were the most acceptable to Marner, for they were rendered without any show of bustling instruction. Silas had shown her the half guinea given to him by Godfrey, and had asked her what he should do about getting some clothes for the child.

"Eh, Master Marner," said Dolly, "there's no call to buy no more nor a pair o' shoes, for I've got the little petticoats as Aaron wore five years ago, and it's ill spending the money on them baby clothes, for the child 'ull grow like grass i' May, bless it—that it will."

And the same day Dolly brought her bundle and displayed to Marner, one by one, the tiny garments in their due order of succession, most of them patched and darned, but clean and neat as fresh-sprung herbs. This was the introduction to a great ceremony with soap and water, from which Baby came out in new beauty and sat on Dolly's knee, handling her toes and chuckling and patting her palms together with an air of having made several discoveries about herself, which she communicated by alternate sounds of "gug, gug, gug," and "mammy." The "mammy" was not a cry of need or uneasiness; Baby had been used to utter it without expecting either tender sound or touch to follow.

"Anybody 'ud think the angils in Heaven couldn't be prettier," said Dolly, rubbing the golden curls and kissing them. "And to think of its being covered wi' them dirty rags—and the poor mother—froze to death; He took care of it and brought it to your door, Master Marner. The door was open, and it walked in over the snow, like as if it had been a little starved robin. Didn't you say the door was open?"

"Yes," said Silas meditatively. "Yes—the door was open. The money's gone I don't know where, and this is come from I don't know where."

He had not mentioned to anyone his unconsciousness of the child's entrance, shrinking from questions which might lead to the fact he himself suspected—namely, that he had been in one of his trances.

"Ah," said Dolly, with soothing gravity, "it's like the night and the morning, and the sleeping and the waking, and the rain and the harvest—one goes and the other comes, and we know nothing how nor where. We may strive and scratch and fend, but it's little we can do arter all—the big things come and go wi' no striving o' our'n—they do, that they do; and I think you're in the right on it to keep the little un, Master Marner, seeing as it's been sent to you, though there's folks as thinks different. You'll happen to be a bit mothering with it while it's so little; but I'll come, and welcome, and see to it for you. I've a bit o' time to spare most days, for when one gets up betimes i' the morning, the clock seems to stan' still tow'rt ten, afore it's time to go about the victual. So, as I say, I'll come and see to the child for you, and welcome."

"Thank you—kindly," said Silas hesitating a little. "I'll be glad if you'll tell me things. But," he added uneasily, leaning forward to look at Baby with some jealousy, as she was resting her head backward against Dolly's arm and eyeing him contentedly from a distance,

"I want to do things for her myself, else she may get fond o' somebody else, and not fond o' me. I've been used to fending for myself in the house—I can learn, I can learn."

"Eh, to be sure," said Dolly gently. "I've seen men as are wonderful handy wi' children. The men are awk'ard and contrairy mostly, God help 'em—but some aren't unsensible. You see this goes first, next the skin," proceeded Dolly, taking up the little shirt and putting it on.

"Yes," said Marner docilely, bringing his eyes very close that they might be initiated in the mysteries; whereupon Baby seized his head with both her small arms and put her lips against his face with purring noises.

"See there," said Dolly with a woman's tender tact, "she's fondest o' you. She wants to go o' your lap, I'll be bound. Go, then. Take her, Master Marner; you can put the things on, and then you can say as you've done for her from the first of her coming to you."

Marner took her on his lap, trembling with an emotion mysterious to himself, at something unknown dawning on his life. Thought and feeling were so confused within him that if he had tried to give them utterance, he could only have said that the child was come instead of the gold—that the gold had turned into the child. He took the garments from Dolly and put them on under her teaching, interrupted, of course, by Baby's gymnastics.

"There, then! Why, you take to it quite easy, Master Marner," said Dolly, "but what shall you do when you're forced to sit at your loom? She'll get busier and mischievouser every day—she will, bless her. It's lucky you've got that high hearth i'stead of a grate, for that keeps the fire more out of her reach; but if you've got anything as can be spilt or broke, or as is fit to cut

140

her fingers off, she'll be at it—and it is but right you should know."

Silas meditated a little while in some perplexity. "I'll tie her to the leg o' the loom," he said at last, "tie her with a good long strip o' something."

"Well, mayhap that'll do, as it's a little gell, for they're easier persuaded to sit i' one place nor the lads. I know what the lads are; for I've had four—four I've had and if you was to take and tie 'em up, they'd make a fighting and crying as if you was ringing the pigs. But I'll bring you my little chair and some bits o' red rag and things for her to play wi', an' she'll sit and chatter to 'em as if they was alive. Eh, if it wasn't a sin to the lads to wish 'em made different, bless 'em, I should ha' been glad for one of 'em to be a little gell. And to think as I could ha' taught her to scour, and mend, and the knitting, and everything. I can teach 'em to this little un, Master Marner, when she gets old enough."

"But she'll be *my* little un," said Marner rather hastily. "She'll be nobody else's."

"No, to be sure; you'll have a right to her, if you're a father to her and bring her up according. But," added Dolly, coming to a point which she had determined beforehand to touch upon, "you must bring her up like christened folks's children, and take her to church, and let her learn her Scriptures, as my little Aaron can say off—the 'I believe,' and everything, and 'hurt nobody by word or deed,' as well as if he was the clerk. That's what you must do, Master Marner, if you'd do the right thing by the orphin child."

Marner's pale face flushed suddenly under a new anxiety. His mind was too busy trying to give some definite bearing to Dolly's words for him to think of answering her.

"And it's my belief," she went on, "as the poor little creature has never been christened, and it's nothing but

141

right as the parson should be spoke to; and if you was noways unwilling, I'd talk to Mr. Macey about it this very day. If the child ever went anyways wrong, and you hadn't done your part by it, Master Marner— 'noculation, and everything to save it from harm—it 'ud be a thorn i' your bed forever o' this side the grave. I can't think as it 'ud be easy lying down for anybody when they'd got to another world, if they hadn't done their part by the helpless children as come wi'out their own asking."

Dolly herself was disposed to be silent for some time now, for she had spoken from the depths of her own simple belief and was much concerned to know whether her words would produce the desired effect on Silas. He was puzzled and anxious, for Dolly's word "christened" conveyed no distinct meaning to him. He had only heard of baptism and had only seen the baptism of grown-up men and women.

"What is it as you mean by 'christened'?" he said at last, timidly. "Won't folks be good to her without it?"

"Dear, dear! Master Marner," said Dolly, with gentle distress and compassion. "Had you never no father nor mother as taught you to say your prayers and as there's good words and good things to keep us from harm?"

"Yes," said Silas in a low voice, "I know a deal about that—used to, used to. But your ways are different; my country was a good way off." He paused a few moments, and then added more decidedly, "I want to do everything as can be done for the child. And whatever's right for her i' this country, and if you think 'ull do her good, I'll act according if you'll tell me."

"Well, then, Master Marner," said Dolly inwardly rejoiced, "I'll ask Mr. Macey to speak to the parson about it. You must fix on a name for her, because she must have a name giv' her when she's christened."

"My mother's name was Hephzibah," said Silas, "and my little sister was named after her."

"Eh, that's a hard name," said Dolly. "I partly think it isn't a christened name."

"It's a Bible name," said Silas, old ideas recurring.

"Then I've no call to speak again' it," said Dolly, rather startled by Silas's knowledge on this, "but you see I'm no scholard, and I'm slow at catching the words. My husband says I'm allays like as if I was putting the haft for the handle—that's what he says—for he's very sharp, God help him. It was awk'ard calling your little sister by such a hard name when you'd got nothing big to say like—wasn't it, Master Marner?"

"We called her Eppie," said Silas.

"Well, if it was noways wrong to shorten the name, it 'ud be a deal handier. So I'll go now, Master Marner, and I'll speak about the christening afore dark. I wish you the best, and it's my belief as it'll come to you, if you do what's right by the orphin child; and there's the 'noculation to be seen to. As to washing its bits o' things, you need look to nobody but me, for I can do 'em wi' one hand when I've got my suds about. Eh, the blessed angil! You'll let me bring my Aaron one of these days, and he'll show her his little cart as his father's made for him, and the black and white pup as he's got a-rearing."

Baby *was* christened, the rector deciding that a double baptism was the lesser risk to incur; and on this occasion Silas, making himself as clean and tidy as he could, appeared for the first time within the church and shared in the observances held sacred by his neighbors. He was quite unable by means of anything he heard or saw to identify the Raveloe religion with his old faith. If he could at any time in his previous life have done so, it must have been by the aid of a strong feeling ready to vibrate with sympathy, rather than by a comparison of phrases and ideas. Now, for long years, that feeling had been dormant. He had no distinct idea about the baptism and the churchgoing except that Dolly had said it was for the good of the child. In this way, as the weeks grew to months, the child created fresher and fresher links between this life and the lives from which he had hitherto shrunk continually into narrower isolation. Unlike the gold, which needed nothing and must be worshiped in close-locked solitude—which was hidden away from the daylight, was deaf to the song of birds, and started to no human tones—Eppie was a creature of endless claims and ever-growing desires, seeking and loving sunshine, and living sounds, and living movements; making trial of everything, with trust in new joy, and stirring the human kindness in all eyes that looked on her. The gold had kept his thoughts in an ever-repeated circle, leading to nothing beyond itself; but Eppie was an object compacted of changes and hopes that forced his thoughts onward and carried them far away from their old eager pacing toward the same blank limit—carried them away to the new things that would come with the coming years when Eppie would have learned to understand how her father Silas cared for her, and made him look for images of that time in the ties and charities that bound together the families of his neighbors. The gold had asked that he should sit weaving longer and longer, deafened and blinded more and more to all things except the monotony of his loom and the repetition of his web; but Eppie called him away from his weaving and made him think all its pauses a holiday, reawakening his senses with her fresh life, even to the old winter flies that came crawling forth in the early spring sunshine, and warming him into joy because *she* had joy.

And when the sunshine grew strong and lasting, so that the buttercups were thick in the meadows, Silas might be seen in the sunny midday or in the late afternoon when the shadows were lengthening under the hedgerows, strolling out with uncovered head to carry Eppie beyond the stone pit to where the flowers grew. When they reached some favorite bank where he could sit down, Eppie would toddle to pluck the flowers and make remarks to the winged things that murmured happily above the bright petals, calling "Dad-dad's" attention continually by bringing him the flowers. Then she would turn her ear to some sudden bird note, and Silas learned to please her by making signs of hushed stillness so that they might listen for the note to come again. When it came, she set up her small back and laughed with gurgling triumph. Sitting on the banks in this way, Silas began to look for the once familiar herbs again. As the leaves, with their unchanged outline and markings, lay on his palm, there was a sense of crowding remembrances from which he turned away timidly, taking refuge in Eppie's little world that lay lightly on his enfeebled spirit.

As the child's mind was growing into knowledge, his mind was growing into memory. As her life unfolded, his soul, long stupefied in a cold, narrow prison, was unfolding, too, and trembling gradually into full consciousness.

It was an influence which gathered force with every new year. The tones that stirred Silas's heart grew articulate and called for more distinct answers. Shapes and sounds grew clearer for Eppie's eyes and ears, and there was more that "Dad-dad" was imperatively required to notice and account for. Also, by the time Eppie was three years old, she developed a fine capacity for mischief and for devising ingenious ways of being troublesome, which found much exercise, not only for Silas's patience, but for his watchfulness. Sorely was poor Silas puzzled on such occasions by the incompatible demands of love. Dolly Winthrop told him that punishment was good for Eppie, and that, as for rearing a child without making it tingle a little in soft and safe places now and then, it was not to be done.

"To be sure, there's another thing you might do, Master Marner," added Dolly meditatively. "You might shut her up once i' the coalhole. That was what I did wi' Aaron, for I was that silly wi' the youngest lad, and I could never bear to smack him. Not as I could find i' my heart to let him stay i' the coalhole more nor a minute, but it was enough to colly him all over so as he must be new washed and dressed, and it was as good as a rod to him—that was. But I put it upo' your conscience, Master Marner, as there's one of 'em you must choose—ayther smacking or the coalhole—else she'll get so masterful there'll be no holding her."

Silas was impressed with the melancholy truth of this last remark, but his force of mind failed before the only two penal methods open to him, not only because it was painful to him to hurt Eppie, but because he trembled at a moment's contention with her, lest she should love him the less for it. It was clear that Eppie with her short, toddling steps must lead Silas a pretty dance on any fine morning when circumstances favored mischief.

For example: he had wisely chosen a broad strip of linen as a means of fastening her to his loom when he was busy. It made a broad belt round her waist and was long enough to allow her to reach the trundle bed and sit down on it, but it was not long enough for her to attempt any dangerous climbing. One bright summer's morning, Silas had been more engrossed than usual in "setting up" a new piece of work, an occasion on which his scissors were in requisition. These scissors, owing to an especial warning of Dolly's, had been kept carefully out of Eppie's reach, but the click of them had had a peculiar attraction for her ear, and watching the results of that click, she had derived the philosophic lesson that the same cause would produce the same effect. Silas had seated himself at his loom, and the noise of weaving had begun; but he had left his scissors on a ledge that Eppie's arm was long enough to reach. Now, like a small mouse watching her opportunity, she stole quietly from her corner, secured the scissors, and toddled to the bed again, setting up her back as a mode of concealing the fact. She had a distinct intention as to the use of the scissors, and having cut the linen strip in a jagged but effectual manner, in two moments she had run out at the open door where the sunshine was inviting her, while poor Silas believed her to be a better child than usual. It was not until he happened to need his scissors that the terrible fact burst upon him; Eppie had run out by herself—had perhaps fallen into the stone pit. Silas, shaken by the worst fear that could have befallen him, rushed out, calling "Eppie!" and ran eagerly about the unenclosed space, exploring the dry cavities into which she might have fallen, and then gazed with questioning dread at the smooth, red surface of the water. The cold drops stood on his brow. How long had she been out? There was one hope—that she had crept through the stile and got into the fields, where he habitually took her to stroll. The grass was high in the meadow, and there was no descrying her if she were there, except by a close search that would be a trespass on Mr. Osgood's crop. Still, that misdemeanor must be committed; and poor Silas, after peering all around the hedgerows, traversed the grass, beginning with perturbed vision to see Eppie behind every group of red sorrel, and to see her moving always farther off as he approached. The meadow was searched in vain, and he got over the stile into the next field, looking with dying hope toward a small pond which was now reduced to its summer shallowness so as to leave a wide margin of good adhesive mud. Here sat Eppie, discoursing cheerfully, to her own small boot, which she was using as a bucket to convey the water into a deep hoofmark, while her little naked foot was planted comfortably on a cushion of olive-green mud. A redheaded calf was observing her with alarmed doubt through the opposite hedge.

Here was clearly a case of aberration in a christened child that demanded severe treatment, but Silas, overcome with convulsive joy at finding his treasure again, could do nothing but snatch her up and cover her with half-sobbing kisses. It was not until he had carried her home, and had begun to think of the necessary washing, that he recollected the need that he should punish Eppie and "make her remember." The idea that she might run away again and come to harm gave him unusual resolution, and for the first time he determined to try the coalhole—a small closet near the hearth.

"Naughty, naughty Eppie," he suddenly began, holding her on his knee and pointing to her muddy feet and clothes, "naughty to cut with the scissors and run away. Eppie must go into the coalhole for being naughty. Daddy must put her in the coalhole."

He half expected that this would be shock enough, and that Eppie would begin to cry. Instead of that, she began to shake herself on his knee, as if the proposition opened a pleasing novelty. Seeing that he must proceed to extremities, he put her into the coalhole and held the door closed, with a trembling sense that he was using a strong measure. For a moment there was silence, but then came a little cry, "Opy, opy!" and Silas let her out again, saying, "Now Eppie 'ull never be naughty again, else she must go into the coalhole—a black, naughty place."

The weaving must stand still a long while this morning, for now Eppie must be washed and have clean clothes put on, but it was to be hoped that this punishment would have a lasting effect and save time in the future—though, perhaps, it would have been better if Eppie had cried more.

In half an hour she was clean again, and Silas, having turned his back to see what he could do with the linen band, threw it down again with the reflection that Eppie would be good without fastening for the rest of the morning. He turned round again, and was going to place her in her little chair near the loom, when she peeped out at him with black face and hands again, and said, "Eppie in de toalhole!"

This total failure of the coalhole discipline shook Silas's belief in the efficacy of punishment. "She'd take it all for fun," he observed to Dolly, "if I didn't hurt her, and that I can't do, Mrs. Winthrop. If she makes me a bit o' trouble, I can bear it. She's got no tricks but what she'll grow out of."

"Well, that's partly true, Master Marner," said Dolly sympathetically, "and if you can't bring your mind to frighten her off touching things, you must do what you can to keep 'em out of her way. That's what I do wi' the pups as the lads are allays a-rearing. They *will* worry and gnaw—worry and gnaw they will, if it was one's Sunday cap as hung anywhere so they could drag it. They know no difference, God help 'em; it's the pushing o' the teeth as sets 'em on, that's what it is."

So Eppie was reared without punishment, the burden of her misdeeds being borne vicariously by Father Silas. The stone hut was made a soft nest for her, lined with downy patience; and also in the world that lay beyond the stone hut, she knew nothing of frowns and denials.

Although it was difficult to carry her and his yarn or linen at the same time, Silas took her with him in most of his journeys to the farmhouses, unwilling to leave her behind at Dolly Winthrop's, who was always ready to take care of her; and little curly-headed Eppie, the weaver's child, became an object of interest at several outlying homesteads, as well as in the village. Hitherto he had been treated very much as if he had been a useful gnome or brownie—a queer and unaccountable creature, who must necessarily be looked at with wondering curiosity and repulsion, but with whom one would be glad to make all greetings and bargains as brief as possible. He must be dealt with in a propitiatory way, and occasionally have a present of pork or garden stuff to carry home with him, seeing that without him there was no getting the yarn woven. But now Silas met with open, smiling faces and cheerful questioning, as a person whose satisfaction and difficulties could be understood. Everywhere he must sit a little and talk about the child, and words of interest were always ready for him: "Ah, Master Marner, you'll be lucky if she takes the measles soon and easy!"—or, "Why, there isn't many lone men 'ud ha' been wishing to take up with a little un like that; but I reckon the weaving makes you handier than men as do outdoor work—you're partly as handy as a woman, for weaving comes next to spinning." Elderly masters and mistresses, seated observantly in large kitchen armchairs, shook their heads over the difficulties attendant on rearing children and felt Eppie's round arms and legs and pronounced them remarkably firm; they told Silas that, if she turned out well (which, however, there was no telling), it would be a fine thing for him to have a steady lass to do for him when he got helpless. Servant maidens were fond of carrying her out to look at the hens and chickens or to see if any cherries could be shaken down in the orchard; and the small boys and girls approached her slowly, with cautious movement and steady gaze, like little dogs face to face with one of their own kind, till attraction had reached the point at which the soft lips were put out for a kiss. No child was afraid of approaching Silas when Eppie was near him. There was no repulsion around him now, either for young or old, for the little child had come to link him once more with the whole world. There was love between him and the child that blended them into one, and there was love between the child and the world.

Silas began now to think of Raveloe life entirely in relation to Eppie. She must have everything that was good in Raveloe, and he listened docilely that he might come to understand better what this life was, from which, for fifteen years, he had stood aloof as from a strange thing wherewith he could have no communion. The disposition to hoard had been utterly crushed at the very first by the loss of his long-stored gold. The coins he earned afterwards seemed as irrelevant as stones brought to complete a house suddenly buried by an earthquake. The sense of bereavement was too heavy upon him for the old thrill of satisfaction to arise again at the touch of the newly earned coin. And now something had come to replace his hoard which gave a growing purpose to the earnings, drawing his hope and joy continually onward beyond the money.

In old days there were angels who came and took men by the hand and led them away from the city of destruction. We see no white-winged angels now. Yet men are led away from threatening destruction; a hand is put into theirs, which leads them forth gently toward a calm and bright land so that they look no more backward. And the hand may be a little child's.

Chapter 15

There was one person, as you will believe, who watched with keener, though more hidden, interest than any other, the prosperous growth of Eppie under the weaver's care. He dared not do anything that would imply a stronger interest in a poor man's adopted child than could be expected from the kindliness of the young Squire, when a chance meeting suggested a little present to a simple old fellow whom others noticed with good will. But he told himself that the time would come when he might do something toward furthering the welfare of his daughter without incurring suspicion. Was he very uneasy in the meantime at his inability to give his daughter her birthright? I cannot say that he was. The child was being taken care of and would very likely be happy, as people in humble stations often were—happier, perhaps, than those brought up in luxury.

Godfrey Cass's cheek and eye were brighter than ever now. He was so undivided in his aims that he seemed like a man of firmness. No Dunsey had come back; people had made up their minds that he was gone for a soldier or gone "out of the country," and no one cared to be specific in their inquiries on a subject delicate to a respectable family. Godfrey had ceased to see the shadow of Dunsey across his path; and the path now lay straight forward to the accomplishment of his best, longest-cherished wishes. Everybody said Mr. Godfrey had taken the right turn; and it was pretty clear what would be the end of things, for there were not many days in the week that he was not seen riding to The Warrens. Godfrey himself, when he was asked jocosely if the day had been fixed, smiled with the pleasant consciousness of a lover who could say "Yes," if he liked. He felt a reformed man, delivered from temptation, and the vision of his future life seemed to him as a promised land for which he had no cause to fight. He saw himself with all his happiness centered on his own hearth, while Nancy would smile on him as he played with the children.

And that other child, not on the hearth—he would not forget it; he would see that it was well provided for. That was a father's duty.

PART II

Chapter 16

It was a bright autumn Sunday, sixteen years after Silas Marner had found his new treasure on the hearth. The bells of the old Raveloe church were ringing the cheerful peal that told that the morning service was ended; and out of the arched doorway in the tower came slowly, retarded by friendly greetings and questions, the richer parishioners who had chosen this bright Sunday morning as eligible for churchgoing. It was the rural fashion of that time for the more important members of the congregation to depart first, while their humbler neighbors waited and looked on, stroking their bent heads or dropping their curtsies to any large ratepayer who turned to notice them.

Foremost among these advancing groups of well-clad people, there are some whom we shall recognize, in spite of Time, who has laid his hand on them all. The tall, blond man of forty is not much changed in features from the Godfrey Cass of six-and-twenty; he is only fuller in flesh, and has only lost the indefinable look of youth—a loss which is marked even when the eye is undulled and the wrinkles are not yet come. Perhaps the pretty woman, not much younger than he, who is leaning on his arm, is more changed than her husband. The lovely bloom that used to be always on her cheek now comes but fitfully with the fresh morning air or with some strong surprise; yet to all who love human faces best for what they tell of human experience, Nancy's beauty has a heightened interest. Often the soul is ripened into fuller goodness while age has spread an ugly film, so that mere glances can never divine the preciousness of the fruit. The years have not been so cruel to Nancy. The firm yet placid mouth, the clear, veracious glance of the brown eyes, speak now of a nature that has been tested and has kept its highest qualities. Even the costume, with its dainty neatness and purity has more significance now that the coquetries of youth can have nothing to do with it.

Mr. and Mrs. Godfrey Cass (any higher title has died away from Raveloe lips since the old Squire was gathered to his fathers and his inheritance was divided) have turned round to look for the tall, aged man and the plainly dressed woman who are a little behind— Nancy having observed that they must wait for "Father and Priscilla"—and now they all turn into a narrower path leading across the churchyard to a small gate opposite Red House. We will not follow them now, for may there not be some others in this departing congregation whom we should like to see again—some of those who are not likely to be handsomely clad and whom we may not recognize so easily as the master and mistress of Red House?

But it is impossible to mistake Silas Marner. His large, brown eyes seem to have gathered a longer vision, as is the way with eyes that have been shortsighted in early life, and they have a less vague, a more answering gaze. In everything else one sees signs of a frame much enfeebled by the lapse of the sixteen years. The weaver's bent shoulders and white hair give him almost the look of advanced age, though he is not more than five-and-fifty, but there is the freshest blossom of youth close by his side—a blonde, dimpled girl of eighteen, who has vainly tried to chastise her curly auburn hair into smoothness under her brown bonnet. The hair ripples as obstinately as a brooklet under the March breeze, and the little ringlets burst away from the restraining comb behind and show themselves below the bonnet crown. Eppie cannot help being rather vexed about her hair, for there is no other girl in Raveloe who has hair at all like it, and she thinks hair ought to be smooth. She does not like to be blameworthy even in small things; you see how neatly her prayer book is folded in her spotted handkerchief.

That good-looking young fellow, in a new fustian suit, who walks behind her, is not quite sure upon the question of hair in the abstract, when Eppie puts it to him, and thinks that perhaps straight hair is the best in general, but he doesn't want Eppie's hair to be different. She surely divines that there is someone behind her who is thinking about her very particularly and mustering courage to come to her side as soon as they are out in the lane. Else why should she look rather shy and take care not to turn away her head from her father Silas, to whom she keeps murmuring little sentences as to who was at church, and who was not at church, and how pretty the red mountain ash is over the rectory wall!

"I wish *we* had a little garden, Father, with double daisies in it, like Mrs. Winthrop's," said Eppie, when they were out in the lane. "Only they say it 'ud take a deal of digging and bringing fresh soil—and you couldn't do that, could you, Father? Anyhow, I shouldn't like you to do it, for it 'ud be too hard work for you."

"Yes, I could do it, child, if you want a bit o' garden. These long evenings I could work at taking in a little bit o' the waste, just enough for a root or two o' flowers for you. Again, i' the morning, I could have a turn wi' the spade before I sat down to the loom. Why didn't you tell me before as you wanted a bit o' garden?"

"*I* can dig it for you, Master Marner," said the young man in fustian, who was now by Eppie's side, entering into the conversation without the trouble of formalities. "It'll be play to me after I've done my day's work, or any off bits o' time when the work's slack. And I'll bring you some soil from Mr. Cass's garden—he'll let me, and willing."

"Eh, Aaron, my lad, are you there?" said Silas. "I wasn't aware of you, for when Eppie's talking o' things, I see nothing but what she's a-saying. Well, if you could help me with the digging, we might get her a bit o' garden all the sooner."

"Then, if you think well and good," said Aaron, "I'll come to Stone Pit this afternoon, and we'll settle what land's to be taken in, and I'll get up an hour earlier i' the morning and begin on it."

"But not if you don't promise me not to work at the hard digging, Father," said Eppie. "For I shouldn't ha' said anything about it," she added, half bashfully, half roguishly, "only Mrs. Winthrop said as Aaron 'ud be so good, and—"

"And you might ha' known it without her telling you," said Aaron. "And Master Marner knows too, I hope, as I'm able and willing to do a turn o' work for him, and he won't do me the unkindness to anyways take it out o' my hands."

"There, now, Father, you won't work in it till it's all easy," said Eppie, "and you and me can mark out the beds, and make holes, and plant the roots. It'll be a deal livelier at Stone Pit when we've got some flowers, for I always think the flowers can see us and know what we're talking about. I'll have a bit of rosemary, and bergamot, and thyme, because they're so sweet-smelling; but there's no lavender only in the gentlefolks' gardens, I think."

"That's no reason why you shouldn't have some," said Aaron, "for I can bring you slips of anything. I'm forced to cut no end of 'em when I'm gardening, and I throw 'em away mostly. There's a big bed o' lavender at Red House. The missus is very fond of it."

"Well," said Silas gravely, "so as you don't make free for us, or ask for anything as is worth much at Red House, for Mr. Cass's been so good to us, and built us up the new end o' the cottage, and given us beds and things, as I couldn't abide to be imposin' for garden stuff or anything else."

"No, no, there's no imposin'," said Aaron. "There's never a garden in all the parish but what there's endless waste in it for want o' somebody as could use everything up. It's what I think to myself sometimes, as there need nobody run short o' victuals if the land was made the most on, and there was never a morsel but what could find its way to a mouth. It sets one thinking o' that—gardening does. But I must go back now, else Mother'll be in trouble as I aren't there."

"Bring her with you this afternoon, Aaron," said Eppie, "I shouldn't like to fix about the garden and her not know everything from the first—should *you*, Father?"

"Ay, bring her if you can, Aaron," said Silas. "She's sure to have a word to say as 'ull help us to set things on their right end."

Aaron turned back up the village, while Silas and Eppie went on up the lonely, sheltered lane.

"Oh, Daddy!" she began when they were in privacy, clasping and squeezing Silas's arm, and skipping round to give him an energetic kiss. "My little, old daddy! I'm so glad. I don't think I shall want anything else when we've got a little garden; and I knew Aaron would dig it for us," she went on with roguish triumph—"I knew that very well."

"You're a deep, little puss, you are," said Silas with the mild, passive happiness of love-crowned age in his face, "but you'll make yourself fine and beholden to Aaron."

"Oh, no, I shan't," said Eppie, laughing and frisking; "he likes it."

"Come, come, let me carry your prayer book, else you'll be dropping it, jumping i' that way."

Eppie was now aware that her behavior was under observation, but it was only the observation of a friendly donkey, browsing with a log fastened to his foot—a meek donkey, not scornfully critical of human trivialities, but thankful to share in them, if possible, by

159

getting his nose scratched. Eppie did not fail to gratify him with her usual notice, though it was attended with the inconvenience of his following them, painfully, up to the very door of their home.

The sound of a sharp bark inside, as Eppie put the key in the door, modified the donkey's views, and he limped away again without bidding. The sharp bark was the sign of an excited welcome that was awaiting them from a knowing brown terrier, who, after dancing at their legs in a hysterical manner, rushed with a worrying noise at a tortoise-shell kitten under the loom and then rushed back with a sharp bark again, as much as to say, "I have done my duty by this feeble creature, you perceive." The lady mother of the kitten sat sunning her white bosom in the window and looked round with a sleepy air of expecting caresses, though she was not going to take any trouble for them.

The presence of this happy animal life was not the only change which had come over the interior of the stone cottage. There was no bed now in the living room, and the small space was well filled with decent furniture, all bright and clean enough to satisfy Dolly Winthrop's eye. The oaken table and three-cornered oaken chair were hardly what was likely to be seen in so poor a cottage. They had come, with the beds and other things, from Red House, for Mr. Godfrey Cass, as everyone said in the village, did very kindly by the weaver. It was nothing but right a man should be looked on and helped by those who could afford it, when he had brought up an orphan child, and been father and mother to her—and had lost his money, too, so as he had nothing but what he worked for week by week, and when the weaving was going down, too—for there was less and less flax spun—and Master Marner was none so young. Nobody was jealous of the weaver, for he was regarded as an exceptional person, whose claims on neighborly help were not to be matched in Raveloe. Any superstition that remained concerning him had taken an entirely new color. Mr. Macey, now a very feeble old man of fourscore and six, never seen except in his chimney corner or sitting in the sunshine at his doorsill, was of opinion that when a man had done what Silas had done by an orphan child, it was a sign that his money would come to light again, or leastwise that the robber would be made to answer for it—for, as Mr. Macey observed of himself, his faculties were as strong as ever.

Silas sat down now and watched Eppie with a satisfied gaze as she spread the clean cloth and set on it the potato pie, warmed up slowly in a safe Sunday fashion by being put into a dry pot over a slowly dying fire as the best substitute for an oven. Silas would not consent to have a grate and oven added to his conveniences; he loved the old brick hearth as he had loved his brown pot—and was it not there when he had found Eppie?

Silas ate his dinner more silently than usual, soon laying down his knife and fork and watching half abstractedly Eppie's play with Snap and the cat, by which her own dining was made rather a lengthy business. It was a sight that might well arrest wandering thoughts—Eppie, with the rippling radiance of her hair and the whiteness of her rounded chin and throat set off by the dark blue cotton gown. Laughing merrily, the kitten held on with her four claws to one shoulder, like a design for a jug handle, while Snap on the right hand and Puss on the other put up their paws toward a morsel that she held out of the reach of both—Snap occasionally desisting in order to remonstrate with the cat by a cogent worrying growl on the greediness and futility of her conduct. Eppie relented, caressed them both, and divided the morsel between them.

At last, Eppie, glancing at the clock, checked the play and said, "Oh, Daddy! You're wanting to go into the sunshine and sit. I must clear away first, so as the house may be tidy when godmother comes. I'll make haste—I won't be long."

Silas had taken to relaxing by the fire. This humble sort of acquiescence had become a strong habit of that new self that had been developed in him since he had found Eppie on his hearth; it had been the only clue his bewildered mind could hold by in cherishing this young life that had been sent to him out of the darkness into which his gold had departed. By seeking what was needful for Eppie, by sharing the effect that everything produced on her, he had himself come to appropriate the forms of custom and belief which were the mold of Raveloe life. As, with reawakening sensibilities, memory also reawakened, he had begun to ponder over the elements of his old faith and blend them with his new impressions till he recovered a consciousness of unity between his past and present. The sense of presiding goodness and the human trust that come with all pure peace and joy had given him a dim impression that there had been some error, some mistake, which had thrown that dark shadow over the days of his best years. As it grew more and more easy to him to open his mind to Dolly Winthrop, he gradually communicated to her all he could describe of his early life. The communication was necessarily a slow and difficult process, for Silas's meager power of explanation was not aided by any readiness of interpretation in Dolly, whose narrow outward experience gave her no key to strange customs and made every novelty a source of wonder that arrested them at every step of the narrative. It was only by fragments, and at intervals which left Dolly time to revolve what she had heard till it acquired some familiarity for her, that Silas at last arrived at the climax of the sad story—the drawing of lots and its false testimony concerning him; and this had to be repeated in several interviews, under new questions on her part as to the nature of this plan for detecting the guilty and clearing the innocent.

"And yourn's the same Bible. You're sure o' that, Master Marner—the Bible as you brought wi' you from that country—it's the same as what they've got at church, and what Eppie's a-learning to read in?"

"Yes," said Silas, "every bit the same; and there's drawing o' lots in the Bible, mind you," he added in a lower tone.

"Oh, dear, dear," said Dolly in a grieved voice, as if she were hearing an unfavorable report of a sick man's case. She was silent for some minutes. At last she said:

"There's wise folks, happen, as know how it all is; the parson knows, I'll be bound; but it takes big words to tell them things, and such as poor folks can't make much out on. I can never rightly know the meaning o' what I hear at church, only a bit here and there, but I know it's good words—I do. What lies upo' your mind—it's this, Master Marner: as, if the One above had done the right thing by you, He'd never ha' let you be turned out for a wicked thief when you was innicent."

"Ah!" said Silas, who had now come to understand Dolly's phraseology. "That was what fell on me like as if it had been red-hot iron; because, you see, it seemed there was nobody as cared for me or clave to me above nor below. And him as I'd gone out and in wi' for ten year and more, since when we was lads and went halves—mine own familiar friend in whom I trusted, had lifted up his heel again' me, and worked to ruin me."

"Eh, but he was a bad un—I can't think as there's another such," said Dolly. "But I'm o'ercome, Master

Marner. I'm like as if I'd waked and didn't know whether it was night or morning. I can make nothing o' the drawing o' lots and the answer coming wrong; it 'ud mayhap take the parson to tell that, and he could only tell us i' big words. What comes to me is if them as prayed and drawed the lots, all but that wicked un, if *they* done the right thing by you, isn't it maybe that He knows better and has a better will? And that's all as ever I can be sure on, and everything else is a big puzzle to me when I think on it. All as we've got to do is to trusten, Master Marner—to do the right thing as fur as we know and to trusten. For if us as knows so little can see a bit 'o good and rights, we may be sure as there's a good and a rights bigger nor what we can know—I feel it i' my own inside as it must be so. And if you could but ha' gone on trustening, Master Marner, you wouldn't ha' run away from your fellow creatures and been so lone."

"Ah, but that 'ud ha' been hard," said Silas, in an undertone; "it 'ud ha' been hard to trusten then."

"And so it would," said Dolly, almost with compunction; "them things are easier said nor done; and I'm partly ashamed o' talking."

"Nay, nay," said Silas, "you're i' the right, Mrs. Winthrop—you're i' the right. There's good i' this world—I've a feeling o' that now; and it makes a man feel as there's a good more nor he can see, i' spite o' the trouble and the wickedness. That drawing o' the lots is dark; but the child was sent to me; there's dealings with us—there's dealings."

This dialogue took place in Eppie's earlier years, when Silas had to part with her for two hours every day that she might learn to read at the dame school, after he had vainly tried himself to guide her in that first step to learning. Now that she was grown up, Silas had often been led, in those moments of quiet outpouring that come to people who live together in perfect love, to talk with *her*, too, of the past, and how and why he had lived a lonely man until she had been sent to him. For it would have been impossible for him to hide from Eppie that she was not his own child. Even if the most delicate reticence on the point could have been expected from Raveloe gossips in her presence, her own questions about her mother could not have been parried, as she grew up, without that complete shrouding of the past which would have made a painful barrier between their minds. So Eppie had long known how her mother had died on the snowy ground, and how she herself had been found on the hearth by Silas, who had taken her golden curls for his lost guineas brought back to him. The tender and peculiar love with which Silas had reared her in almost inseparable companionship with himself, aided by the seclusion of their dwelling, had preserved her from the lowering influences of the village talk and habits, and had kept her mind in that freshness which is sometimes falsely supposed to be an invariable attribute of rusticity. Perfect love has a breath of poetry which can exalt the relations of the least-instructed human beings. This breath of poetry had surrounded Eppie from the time when she had followed the bright gleam that beckoned her to Silas's hearth. It is not surprising if in other things besides her delicate prettiness she was not quite a common village maiden, but had a touch of refinement and fervor which came from no other teaching than that of tenderly nurtured, unvitiated feeling. She was too childish and simple for her imagination to rove into questions about her unknown father. For a long while it did not even occur to her that she must have had a father, and the first time that the idea of her mother having had a husband presented itself to her was when Silas showed her the wedding ring which had been taken from the wasted finger, and had been carefully preserved by him in a little lacquered box shaped like a shoe. He delivered this box into Eppie's charge when she had grown up, and she often opened it to look at the ring. Still she thought hardly at all about the father of whom it was the symbol. Had she not a father very close to her, who loved her better than any real fathers in the village seemed to love their daughters? On the contrary, who her mother was, and how she came to die in that forlornness, were questions that often pressed on Eppie's mind. Her knowledge of Mrs. Winthrop, who was her nearest friend next to Silas, made her feel that a mother must be very precious. She had again and again asked Silas to tell her how her mother looked, whom she was like, and how he had found her against the furze bush, led toward it by the little footsteps and the outstretched arms. The furze bush was there still, and this afternoon when Eppie came out with Silas into the sunshine, it was the first object that arrested her eyes and thoughts.

"Father," she said in a tone of gentle gravity, which sometimes came like a sadder, slower cadence across her playfulness, "we shall take the furze bush into the garden. It'll come into the corner, and just against it I'll put snowdrops and crocuses, 'cause Aaron says they won't die out, but'll always get more and more."

"Ah, child," said Silas, "it wouldn't do to leave out the furze bush. There's nothing prettier to my thinking, when it's yallow with flowers. It's just come into my head what we're to do for a fence—mayhap Aaron can help us. A fence we must have, else the donkeys and things 'ull come and trample everything down. And fencing's hard to be got at, by what I can make out."

"Oh, I'll tell you, Daddy," said Eppie, clasping her hands suddenly, after a minute's thought. "There's lots o' loose stones about, some of 'em not big, and we might lay 'em atop of one another and make a wall. You and me could carry the smallest, and Aaron 'ud carry the rest—I know he would."

"Eh, my precious un," said Silas, "there isn't enough stones to go all round; and as for you carrying, why, wi' your little arms you couldn't carry a stone no bigger than a turnip. You're dillicate made, my dear," he added with a tender intonation. "That's what Mrs. Winthrop says."

"Oh, I'm stronger than you think, Daddy," said Eppie, "and if there wasn't stones enough to go all round, why they'll go part o' the way, and then it'll be easier to get sticks and things for the rest. See here, round the big pit, what a many stones!"

She skipped forward to the pit, meaning to lift one of the stones and exhibit her strength, but she started back in surprise.

"Oh, Father, just come and look here," she exclaimed. "Come and see how the water's gone down since yesterday. Why, yesterday the pit was ever so full!"

"Well, to be sure," said Silas coming to her side. "Why, that's the draining they've begun on, since harvest i' Mr. Osgood's fields, I reckon. The foreman said to me the other day when I passed by 'em, 'Master Marner,' he said, 'I shouldn't wonder if we lay your bit o' waste as dry as a bone.' It was Mr. Godfrey Cass, he said, had gone into the draining; he'd been taking these fields o' Mr. Osgood."

"How odd it'll seem to have the old pit dried up!" said Eppie, turning away and stooping to lift rather a large stone. "See, Daddy, I can carry this quite well," she said, going along with much energy for a few steps, but presently letting it fall.

"Ah, you're fine and strong, aren't you?" said Silas, while Eppie shook her aching arms and laughed. "Come, come, let us go and sit down on the bank against the stile there and have no more lifting. You might hurt yourself, child. You need have somebody to work for you—and my arm isn't overstrong."

Silas uttered the last sentence slowly, as if it implied more than met the ear, and Eppie, when they sat down on the bank, nestled close to his side, and, taking hold caressingly of the arm that was not overstrong, held it on her lap: An ash in the hedgerow behind made a fretted screen from the sun and threw happy, playful shadows all about them.

"Father," said Eppie very gently, after they had been sitting in silence a little while, "if I was to be married, ought I to be married with my mother's ring?"

Silas gave an almost imperceptible start, though the question fell in with the undercurrent of thought in his own mind. Then, in a subdued tone, "Why, Eppie, have you been a-thinking on it?"

"Only this last week, Father," said Eppie ingenuously, "since Aaron talked to me about it."

"And what did he say?" said Silas, still in the same subdued way, as if he were anxious lest he should fall into the slightest tone that was not for Eppie's good.

"He said he should like to be married, because he was a-going on four-and-twenty and had got a deal of gardening work, now Mr. Mott's given up, and he goes twice a-week regular to Mr. Cass's and once to Mr. Osgood's, and they're going to take him on at the rectory."

"And who is it as he's wanting to marry?" said Silas with rather a sad smile.

"Why, me, to be sure, Daddy," said Eppie, with dimpling laughter, kissing her father's cheek. "As if he'd want to marry anybody else!"

"And you mean to have him, do you?" said Silas.

"Yes, sometime," said Eppie, "I don't know when. Everybody's married sometime, Aaron says. But I told

168

him that wasn't true; for, I said, look at Father—he's never been married."

"No, child," said Silas, "your father was a lone man till you was sent to him."

"But you'll never be lone again, Father," said Eppie tenderly. "That was what Aaron said—'I could never think o' taking you away from Master Marner, Eppie.' And I said, 'It 'ud be no use if you did, Aaron.' He wants us all to live together, so as you needn't work a bit, Father, only what's for your own pleasure, and he'd be as good as a son to you—that was what he said."

"Would you like that, Eppie?" said Silas, looking at her.

"I shouldn't mind it, Father," said Eppie quite simply. "And I should like things to be so as you needn't work much. If it wasn't for that, I'd sooner things didn't change. I'm very happy. I like Aaron to be fond of me, and come and see us often, and behave pretty to you—he always *does* behave pretty to you, doesn't he, Father?"

"Yes, child, nobody could behave better," said Silas emphatically. "He's his mother's lad."

"But I don't want any change," said Eppie. "I should like to go on a long, long while, just as we are. Only Aaron does want a change; and he made me cry a bit—only a bit—because he said I didn't care for him, for if I cared for him I should want us to be married, as he did."

"Eh, my blessed child," said Silas, "you're o'er young to be married. We'll ask Mrs. Winthrop—we'll ask Aaron's mother what *she* thinks. If there's a right thing to do, she'll come at it. There's this to be thought on, Eppie: things *will* change, whether we like it or no. Things won't go on for a long while just as they are and no difference. I shall get older and helplesser and be a burden on you, belike, if I don't go away from you altogether. Not as I mean you'd think me a burden—I know you wouldn't—but it 'ud be hard upon you. When I look for'ard to that, I like to think as you'd have somebody else besides me—somebody young and strong—as'll outlast your own life, and take care on you to the end." Silas paused and, resting his wrists on his knees, lifted his hands up and down meditatively as he looked on the ground.

"Then, would you like me to be married, Father?" said Eppie, with a little trembling in her voice.

"I'll not be the man to say no, Eppie," said Silas emphatically, "but we'll ask your godmother. She'll wish the right thing by you and her son too."

"There they come, then," said Eppie. "Let us go and meet 'em."

Chapter 17

While Silas and Eppie were seated on the bank discoursing in the fleckered shade of the ash tree, Miss Priscilla Lammeter was resisting her sister's arguments that it would be better to take tea at Red House, and let her father have a long nap, than drive home to The Warrens so soon after dinner. The family party (of four only) were seated round the table in the dark wainscoted parlor, with the Sunday dessert before them, of fresh filberts, apples, and pears, duly ornamented with leaves by Nancy's own hand before the bells had rung for church.

A great change has come over the dark wainscoted parlor since we saw it in Godfrey's bachelor days under the wifeless reign of the old Squire. Now all is polish, on which no yesterday's dust is ever allowed to rest, from the yard's width of oaken boards round the carpet, to the old Squire's guns and whips and walking sticks, ranged on the stag's antlers above the mantelpiece. All other signs of sporting and outdoor occupation Nancy has removed to another room, but she has brought into Red House the habit of filial reverence and preserves sacredly in a place of honor these relics of her husband's departed father. The tankards are on the side table still, but the bossed silver is undimmed by handling, and there are no dregs to send forth unpleasant suggestions; the only prevailing scent is of the lavender and rose leaves that fill the vases of Derbyshire spar. All is purity and order in this once dreary room, for, fifteen years ago it was entered by a new presiding spirit.

"Now, Father," said Nancy, "*is* there any call for you to go home to tea? Mayn't you just as well stay with us?—such a beautiful evening as it's likely to be."

The old gentleman had been talking with Godfrey

about the increasing poor rate and the ruinous times and had not heard the dialogue between his daughters.

"My dear, you must ask Priscilla," he said, in the once firm voice, now become rather broken. "She manages me and the farm too."

"And reason good as I should manage you, Father," said Priscilla, "else you'd be giving yourself your death with rheumatism. As for the farm, if anything turns out wrong, as it can't but do in these times, there's nothing kills a man so soon as having nobody to find fault with but himself. It's a deal the best way o' being master, to let somebody else do the ordering and keep the blaming in your own hands. It 'ud save many a man a stroke, *I* believe."

"Wel., well, my dear," said her father with a quiet laugh, "I didn't say you don't manage for everybody's good."

"Then manage so as you may stay to tea, Priscilla," said Nancy, putting her hand on her sister's arm affectionately. "Come now, and we'll go round the garden while Father has his nap."

"My dear child, he'll have a beautiful nap in the gig, for I shall drive. As for staying to tea, I can't hear of it, for there's this dairymaid, now she knows she's to be married, she'd as lief pour the new milk into the pig trough as into the pans. That's the way with 'em all. It's as if they thought the world 'ud be new-made because they're to be married. So come and let me put my bonnet on, and there'll be time for us to walk round the garden while the horse is being put in."

When the sisters were treading the neatly swept garden walks, between the bright turf that contrasted pleasantly with the dark cones and arches and wall-like hedges of yew, Priscilla said:

"I'm as glad as anything at your husband's making that exchange o' land with Cousin Osgood and beginning the dairying. It's a thousand pities you didn't do it before, for it'll give you something to fill your mind. There's nothing like a dairy if folks want a bit o' worrit to make the days pass. As for rubbing furniture, when you can once see your face in a table, there's nothing else to look for, but there's always something fresh with the dairy. Even in the depths o' winter, there's some pleasure in conquering the butter and making it come whether or no. My dear," added Priscilla, pressing her sister's hand affectionately as they walked side by side, "you'll never be low when you've got a dairy."

"Ah, Priscilla," said Nancy, returning the pressure with a grateful glance of her clear eyes, "but it won't make up to Godfrey; a dairy's not so much to a man. It's only what he cares for that ever makes me low. I'm contented with the blessings we have, if he could be contented."

"It drives me past patience," said Priscilla impetuously, "that way o' the men—always wanting and wanting and never easy with what they've got. They can't sit comfortable in their chairs when they've neither ache nor pain. Joyful be it spoken, our father was never that sort o' man. If it had pleased God to make you ugly, like me, so as the men wouldn't ha' run after you, we might have kept to our own family and had nothing to do with folks as have got uneasy blood in their veins."

"Oh, don't say so, Priscilla," said Nancy, repenting that she had called forth this outburst. "Nobody has any occasion to find fault with Godfrey. It's natural he should be disappointed at not having any children. Every man likes to have somebody to work for and lay by for, and he always counted so on making a fuss with 'em when they were little. There's many another man 'ud hanker more than he does. He's the best of husbands."

"Oh, I know," said Priscilla, smiling sarcastically. "I know the way o' wives; they set one on to abuse their husbands, and then they turn round on one and praise 'em as if they wanted to sell 'em. But Father'll be waiting for me; we must turn now."

The large gig with the steady old gray was at the front door, and Mr. Lammeter was already on the stone steps, passing the time in recalling to Godfrey what very fine points Speckle had when his master used to ride him.

"I always *would* have a good horse, you know," said the old gentleman, not liking that spirited time to be quite effaced from the memory of his juniors.

"Mind you bring Nancy to The Warrens before the week's out, Mr. Cass," was Priscilla's parting injunction, as she took the reins and shook them gently, by way of friendly incitement to Speckle.

"I shall just take a turn to the fields against the stone pit, Nancy, and look at the draining," said Godfrey.

"You'll be in again by tea time, dear?"

"Oh, yes, I shall be back in an hour."

It was Godfrey's custom on a Sunday afternoon to do a little contemplative farming in leisurely walk. Nancy seldom accompanied him; for the women of her generation—unless, like Priscilla, they took to outdoor management—were not given to much walking beyond their own house and garden, finding sufficient exercise in domestic duties. So, when Priscilla was not with her, she usually sat with her Bible before her, and after following the text with her eyes for a little while, she would gradually permit them to wander as her thoughts had already insisted on wandering.

There was one main thread of painful experience in Nancy's married life, and on it hung certain deeply felt scenes, which were the oftenest revived in retrospect. The short dialogue with Priscilla in the garden had determined the current of retrospect in that frequent direction this particular Sunday afternoon. The first wandering of her thought from the text, which she still attempted dutifully to follow with her eyes and silent lips, was into an imaginary enlargement of the defense she had set up for her husband against Priscilla's implied blame. The vindication of the loved object is the best balm affection can find for its wounds. "A man must have so much on his mind," is the belief by which a wife often supports a cheerful face under rough answers and unfeeling words. Nancy's deepest wounds had all come from the perception that the absence of children from their hearth was dwelt on in her husband's mind as a privation to which he could not reconcile himself.

Yet sweet Nancy might have been expected to feel still more keenly the denial of a blessing to which she had looked forward with all the varied expectations and preparations, solemn and prettily trivial, which fill the mind of a loving woman when she expects to become a mother. Was there not a drawer filled with the neat work of her hands, all unworn and untouched, just as she had arranged it there fourteen years ago—just, but for one little dress, which had been made the burial dress? But under this immediate personal trial, Nancy was so firmly unmurmuring that years ago she had suddenly renounced the habit of visiting this drawer, lest she should in this way be cherishing a longing for what was not given.

Perhaps it was this very severity toward any indulgence of what she held to be sinful regret in herself that made her shrink from applying her own standard to her husband. "It is very different—it is much worse for a man to be disappointed in that way. A woman can always be satisfied with devoting herself to her husband, but a man wants something that will make him look forward more—and sitting by the fire is so much duller to him than to a woman." Always, when Nancy reached this point in her meditations—trying, with predetermined sympathy, to see everything as Godfrey saw it—there came a renewal of self-questioning. *Had* she done everything in her power to lighten Godfrey's privation? Had she really been right in the resistance, which had cost her so much pain six years ago, and again four years ago—the resistance to her husband's wish that they should adopt a child? Adoption was more remote from the ideas and habits of that time than of our own. Still, Nancy had her opinion on it. It was as necessary to her mind to have an opinion on all topics, not exclusively masculine, that had come under her notice, as for her to have a precisely marked place for every article of her personal property, and her opinions were always principles to be unwaveringly acted on. They were firm, not because of their basis, but because she held them with a tenacity inseparable from her mental action. On all the duties and proprieties of life, from filial behavior to the arrangements of the evening toilet, pretty Nancy Lammeter, by the time she was three-and-twenty, had her unalterable little code, and had formed every one of her habits in strict accordance with that code. She carried these decided judgments within her in the most unobtrusive way; they rooted themselves in her mind and grew there as quietly as grass. Years ago, we know, she insisted on dressing like Priscilla, because "it was right for sisters to dress alike," and because "she would do what was right if she wore a gown dyed with cheese coloring." That was a trivial but typical instance of the mode in which Nancy's life was regulated.

It was one of those rigid principles, and no petty egotistic feeling that had been the ground of Nancy's difficult resistance to her husband's wish. To adopt a child, because children of your own had been denied you, was to try and choose your lot in spite of Providence. The adopted child, she was convinced, would never turn out well and would be a curse to those who had willfully and rebelliously sought what, for some high reason, they were better without.

"But why should you think the child would turn out ill?" said Godfrey, in his remonstrances. "She has thriven as well as a child can do with the weaver, and *he* adopted her. There isn't such a pretty little girl anywhere else in the parish, or one fitter for the station we could give her. Where can be the likelihood of her being a curse to anybody?"

"Yes, my dear Godfrey," said Nancy, who was sitting with her hands tightly clasped together, and with yearning, regretful affection in her eyes. "The child may not turn out ill with the weaver. But, then, he didn't go to seek her, as we should be doing. It will be wrong; I feel sure it will. Don't you remember what that lady we met at the Royston Baths told us about the child her sister adopted? That was the only adopting I ever heard of; and the child was transported when it was twenty-three. Dear Godfrey, don't ask me to do what I know is wrong; I should never be happy again. I know it's very hard for *you*—it's easier for me—but it's the will of Providence."

Godfrey had from the first specified Eppie, then about twelve years old, as a child suitable for them to adopt. It had never occurred to him that Silas would rather part with his life than with Eppie. Surely the weaver would wish the best to the child he had taken so much trouble with, and would be glad that such good fortune should happen to her. She would always be very grateful to him, and he would be well provided for to the end of his life—provided for as the excellent part he had done by the child deserved. Was it not an appropriate thing for people in a higher station to take a charge off the hands of a lower? It seemed an eminently appropriate thing to Godfrey for reasons that were known only to himself, and by a common fallacy, he imagined the measure would be easy because he had private motives for desiring it.

"I was right," Nancy said to herself, when she had recalled all their scenes of discussion. "I feel I was right to say him nay, though it hurt me more than anything, but how good Godfrey has been about it! Many men would have been very angry with me for standing out against their wishes, and they might have thrown out that they'd had ill luck in marrying me; but Godfrey has never been the man to say me an unkind word. It's only what he can't hide. Everything seems so blank to him, I know; and the land—what difference it 'ud make to him when he goes to see after things if he'd children growing up that he was doing it all for! But I won't murmur, and perhaps if he'd married a woman who'd have had children, she'd have vexed him in other ways."

This possibility was Nancy's chief comfort, and to give it greater strength, she labored to make it impossible that any other wife should have had more perfect tenderness. She had been *forced* to vex him by that one denial. Godfrey was not insensible to her loving effort and did Nancy no injustice as to the motives of her obstinacy. It was impossible to have lived with her fifteen years and not be aware that an unselfish clinging to the right, and a sincerity clear as the flower-born dew, were her main characteristics. Indeed, Godfrey felt this so strongly that his own more wavering nature, too averse to facing difficulty to be unvaryingly simple and truthful, was kept in a certain awe of this gentle wife who watched his looks with a yearning to obey them. It seemed to him impossible that he should ever confess to her the truth about Eppie. She would never recover from the repulsion the story of his earlier marriage would create, told to her now, after that long concealment. The child, too, he thought, must become an object of repulsion. The very sight of her would be painful. The shock of Nancy's mingled pride and ignorance of the world's evil might even be too much for her delicate frame. Since he had married her with that secret on his heart, he must keep it there to the last. Whatever else he did, he could not make an irreparable breach between himself and this long-loved wife.

On this Sunday afternoon, it was already four years since there had been any allusion to the subject between them, and Nancy supposed that it was forever buried.

"I wonder if he'll mind it less or more as he gets older," she thought. "I'm afraid more. Aged people feel the miss of children; what would Father do without Priscilla? And if I die, Godfrey will be very lonely—not holding together with his brothers much. But I won't be overanxious and trying to make things out beforehand. I must do my best for the present."

With that last thought Nancy roused herself from her reverie and turned her eyes again toward the forsaken page. It had been forsaken longer than she imagined, for she was presently surprised by the appearance of the servant with the tea things. It was, in fact, a little before the usual time for tea, but Jane had her reasons.

"Is your master come into the yard, Jane?"

"No'm, he isn't," said Jane with a slight emphasis, of which, however, her mistress took no notice.

"I don't know whether you've seen 'em, 'm," continued Jane after a pause, "but there's folks making haste all one way, afore the front window. I doubt something's happened. There's niver a man to be seen i' the yard, else I'd send and see. I've been up into the top attic, but there's no seeing anything for trees. I hope nobody's hurt, that's all."

"Oh, no, I daresay there's nothing much the matter," said Nancy. "It's perhaps Mr. Snell's bull got out again, as he did before."

"I wish he mayn't gore anybody then, that's all," said Jane, not altogether despising a hypothesis which covered a few imaginary calamities.

"That girl is always terrifying me," thought Nancy. "I wish Godfrey would come in."

She went to the front window and looked as far as she could see along the road, with an uneasiness that she felt to be childish, for there were now no such signs of excitement as Jane had spoken of, and Godfrey would not be likely to return by the village road, but by the fields. She continued to stand, however, looking at the placid churchyard with the long shadows of the gravestones across the bright green hillocks and at the glowing autumn colors of the rectory trees beyond. Before such calm external beauty the presence of a vague fear is more distinctly felt—like a raven flapping its slow wing across the sunny air. Nancy wished more and more that Godfrey would come in.

Chapter 18

Someone opened the door at the other end of the room, and Nancy felt that it was her husband. She turned from the window with gladness in her eyes, for the wife's chief dread was stilled.

"Dear, I'm so thankful you're come," she said, going toward him. "I began to get . . ."

She paused abruptly, for Godfrey was laying down his hat with trembling hands and turned toward her with a pale face and a strange, unanswering glance, as if he saw her indeed, but saw her as part of a scene invisible to herself. She laid her hand on his arm, not daring to speak again, but he left the touch unnoticed and threw himself into his chair.

Jane was already at the door with the hissing urn. "Tell her to keep away, will you?" said Godfrey. When the door was closed again, he exerted himself to speak more distinctly.

"Sit down, Nancy—there," he said, pointing to a chair opposite him. "I came back as soon as I could to hinder anybody's telling you but me. I've had a great shock—but I care most about the shock it'll be to you."

"It isn't Father and Priscilla?" said Nancy with quivering lips, clasping her hands together tightly on her lap.

"No, it's nobody living," said Godfrey, unequal to the considerate skill with which he would have wished to make his revelation. "It's Dunstan—my brother Dunstan, that we lost sight of sixteen years ago. We've found him—found his body—his skeleton."

The deep dread Godfrey's look had created in Nancy made her feel these words a relief. She sat in comparative calmness to hear what else he had to tell. He went on:

"The stone pit has gone dry suddenly—from the draining, I suppose, and there he lies—has lain for sixteen years, wedged between two great stones. There's his watch and seals, and there's my gold-handled hunting whip with my name on. He took it away without my knowing the day he went hunting on Wildfire, the last time he was seen."

Godfrey paused. It was not so easy to say what came next. "Do you think he drowned himself?" said Nancy, almost wondering that her husband should be so deeply shaken by what had happened all those years ago to an unloved brother, of whom worse things had been augured.

"No, he fell in," said Godfrey in a low but distinct voice, as if he felt some deep meaning in the fact. Presently he added, "Dunstan was the man that robbed Silas Marner."

The blood rushed to Nancy's face and neck at this surprise and shame, for she had been bred up to regard even a distant kinship with crime as a dishonor.

"Oh, Godfrey!" she said, with compassion in her tone, for she had immediately reflected that the dishonor must be felt still more keenly by her husband.

"There was the money in the pit," he continued—"all the weaver's money. Everything's been gathered up, and they're taking the skeleton to the Rainbow. But I came back to tell you. There was no hindering it; you must know."

He was silent, looking on the ground for two long minutes. Nancy would have said some words of comfort under this disgrace, but she refrained from an instinctive sense that there was something behind—that Godfrey had something else to tell her. Presently he lifted his eyes to her face and kept them fixed on her as he said:

"Everything comes to light, Nancy, sooner or later. When God Almighty wills it, our secrets are found out. I've lived with a secret on my mind, but I'll keep it from you no longer. I wouldn't have you know it by somebody else, and not by me—I wouldn't have you find it out after I'm dead. I'll tell you now. It's been 'I will' and 'I won't' with me all my life—I'll make sure of myself now."

Nancy's utmost dread had returned. The eyes of the husband and wife met with awe in them, as at a crisis which suspended affection.

"Nancy," said Godfrey slowly, "when I married you, I hid something from you—something I ought to have told you. That woman Marner found dead in the snow—Eppie's mother—that wretched woman—was my wife; Eppie is my child."

He paused, dreading the effect of his confession. Nancy sat quite still, only that her eyes dropped and ceased to meet his. She was pale and quiet as a meditative statue, clasping her hands on her lap.

"You'll never think the same of me again," said Godfrey, after a little while, with some tremor in his voice.

She was silent.

"I oughtn't to have left the child unowned. I oughtn't to have kept it from you; but I couldn't bear to give you up, Nancy. I was led away into marrying her—I suffered for it."

Still Nancy was silent, looking down, and he almost expected that she would presently get up and say she would go to her father's. How could she have any mercy for faults that must seem so black to her, with her simple, severe notions?

At last she lifted up her eyes to his again and spoke. There was no indignation in her voice—only deep regret.

"Godfrey, if you had but told me this six years ago, we could have done some of our duty by the child. Do you think I'd have refused to take her in, if I'd known she was yours?"

At that moment Godfrey felt all the bitterness of an error that was not simply futile, but had defeated its own end. He had not measured this wife with whom he had lived so long. But she spoke again, with more agitation.

"And—oh, Godfrey—if we'd had her from the first, if you'd taken to her as you ought, she'd have loved me for her mother—and you'd have been happier with me; I could better have bore my little baby dying, and our life might have been more like what we used to think it 'ud be."

The tears fell, and Nancy ceased to speak.

"But you wouldn't have married me then, Nancy, if I'd told you," said Godfrey, urged, in the bitterness of his self-reproach, to prove to himself that his conduct had not been utter folly. "You may think you would now, but you wouldn't then. With your pride and your father's, you'd have hated having anything to do with me after the talk there'd have been."

"I can't say what I should have done about that, Godfrey. I should never have married anybody else. But I wasn't worth doing wrong for—nothing is in this world. Nothing is so good as it seems beforehand—not even our marrying wasn't, you see."

"I'm a worse man than you thought I was, Nancy," said Godfrey rather tremulously. "Can you forgive me ever?"

"The wrong to me is but little, Godfrey. You've made it up to me. You've been good to me for fifteen years. It's another you did the wrong to, and I doubt it can ever be all made up."

"But we can take Eppie now," said Godfrey. "I won't mind the world knowing at last. I'll be plain and open for the rest o' my life."

"It'll be different coming to us now she's grown up," said Nancy. "But it's your duty to acknowledge her and provide for her, and I'll do my part by her and pray to God Almighty to make her love me."

"Then we'll go together to Silas Marner's this very night, as soon as everything's quiet at the stone pit."

Chapter 19

Between eight and nine o'clock that evening, Eppie and Silas were seated alone in the cottage. After the great excitement the weaver had undergone from the events of the afternoon, he had felt a longing for this quietude and had even begged Mrs. Winthrop and Aaron, who had naturally lingered behind everyone else, to leave him alone with his daughter. The excitement had not passed away. It had only reached that stage when the keenness of the susceptibility makes external stimulus intolerable—when there is no sense of weariness, but rather an intensity of inward life, under which sleep is an impossibility.

Silas's face showed that sort of transfiguration as he sat in his armchair and looked at Eppie. She had drawn her own chair toward his knees and leaned forward, holding both his hands, while she looked up at him. On the table near them, lit by a candle, lay the recovered gold—the old, long-loved gold, arranged in orderly heaps as Silas used to arrange it in the days when it was his only joy. He had been telling her how he used to count it every night, and how his soul was utterly desolate till she was sent to him.

"At first, I'd a sort o' feeling come across me now and then," he was saying in a subdued tone, "as if you might be changed into the gold again, for sometimes, turn my head which way I would, I seemed to see the gold; and I thought I should be glad if I could feel it and find it was come back. That didn't last long. After a bit, I should have thought it was a curse come again, if it had drove you from me, for I'd got to feel the need o' your looks and your voice and the touch o' your little fingers. You didn't know then, Eppie, when you were such a little un—you didn't know what your old father Silas felt for you."

"But I know now, Father," said Eppie. "If it hadn't been for you, they'd have taken me to the workhouse, and there'd have been nobody to love me."

"Eh, my precious child, the blessing was mine. If you hadn't been sent to save me, I should ha' gone to the grave in my misery. The money was taken away from me in time; and you see it's been kept—kept till it was wanted for you. It's wonderful—our life is wonderful."

Silas sat in silence a few minutes, looking at the money. "It takes no hold of me now," he said ponderingly—"the money doesn't. I wonder if it ever could again—it might if I lost you, Eppie. I might come to think I was forsaken again and lose the feeling that God was good to me."

At that moment there was a knocking at the door, and Eppie was obliged to rise without answering Silas. Beautiful she looked, with the tenderness of gathering tears in her eyes and a slight flush on her cheeks, as she stepped to open the door. The flush deepened when she saw Mr. and Mrs. Godfrey Cass. She made her little rustic curtsy and held the door wide for them to enter.

"We're disturbing you very late, my dear," said Mrs. Cass, taking Eppie's hand and looking in her face with an expression of anxious interest and admiration. Nancy herself was pale and tremulous.

Eppie, after placing chairs for Mr. and Mrs. Cass, went to stand against Silas, opposite to them.

"Well, Marner," said Godfrey trying to speak with perfect firmness, "it's a great comfort to me to see you with your money again, that you've been deprived of so many years. It was one of my family did you the wrong—the more grief to me—and I feel bound to make up to you for it in every way. Whatever I can do for you will be nothing but paying a debt, even if I looked no further than the robbery. But there are other

187

things I'm beholden—shall be beholden to you for, Marner."

Godfrey checked himself. It had been agreed between him and his wife that the subject of his fatherhood should be approached very carefully, and that, if possible, the disclosure should be reserved for the future, so that it might be made to Eppie gradually. Nancy had urged this because she felt strongly the painful light in which Eppie must inevitably see the relation between her father and mother.

Silas, always ill at ease when he was being spoken to by "betters," such as Mr. Cass—tall, powerful, florid men, seen chiefly on horseback—answered with some constraint:

"Sir, I've a deal to thank you for a'ready. As for the robbery, I count it no loss to me. If I did, you couldn't help it. You aren't answerable for it."

"You may look at it in that way, Marner, but I never can, and I hope you'll let me act according to my own feeling of what's just. I know you're easily contented. You've been a hard-working man all your life."

"Yes, sir, yes," said Marner meditatively. "I should ha' been bad off without my work. It was what I held by when everything else was gone from me."

"Ah," said Godfrey, applying Marner's words simply to his bodily wants, "it was a good trade for you in this country, because there's been a great deal of linen-weaving to be done, but you're getting rather past such close work, Marner. It's time you laid by and had some rest. You look a good deal pulled down, though you're not an old man, *are* you?"

"Fifty-five, as near as I can say, sir," said Silas.

"Oh, why, you may live thirty years longer—look at old Macey! And that money on the table, after all, is but little. It won't go far either way—whether it's put out to interest, or you were to live on it as long as it would last. It wouldn't go far if you'd nobody to keep but yourself, and you've had two to keep for a good many years now."

"Eh, sir," said Silas unaffected by anything Godfrey was saying, "I'm in no fear o' want. We shall do very well—Eppie and me 'ull do well enough. There's few workingfolks have got so much laid by as that. I don't know what it is to gentlefolks, but I look upon it as a deal—almost too much. As for us, it's little we want."

"Only the garden, Father," said Eppie, blushing up to the ears the moment after.

"You love a garden, do you, my dear?" said Nancy, thinking that this turn in the point of view might help her husband. "We should agree in that. I give a deal of time to the garden."

"Ah, there's plenty of gardening at Red House," said Godfrey, surprised at the difficulty he found in approaching a proposition that had seemed so easy to him in the distance. "You've done a good part by Eppie, Marner, for sixteen years. It 'ud be a great comfort to you to see her well provided for, wouldn't it? She looks blooming and healthy, but not fit for any hardships. She doesn't look like a strapping girl come of working parents. You'd like to see her taken care of by those who can leave her well off, and make a lady of her; she's more fit for it than for a rough life, such as she might come to in a few years' time."

A slight flush came over Marner's face and disappeared like a passing gleam. Eppie simply wondered why Mr. Cass should talk so about things that seemed to have nothing to do with reality, but Silas was hurt and uneasy.

"I don't take your meaning, sir," he answered, not having words at command to express the mingled feelings with which he had heard Mr. Cass's words.

"Well, my meaning is this, Marner," said Godfrey, determined to come to the point, "Mrs. Cass and I, you know, have no children—nobody to be the better for our good home and everything else we have—more than enough for ourselves. We should like to have somebody in the place of a daughter to us—we should like to have Eppie and treat her in every way as our own child. It 'ud be a great comfort to you in your old age, I hope, to see her fortune made in that way, after you've been at the trouble of bringing her up so well. And it's right you should have every reward for that. Eppie, I'm sure, will always love you and be grateful to you; she'd come and see you very often, and we should all be on the lookout to do everything we could toward making you comfortable."

A plain man like Godfrey Cass, speaking under some embarrassment, necessarily blunders on words that are coarser than his intentions and that are likely to fall gratingly on susceptible feelings. While he had been speaking, Eppie had quietly passed her arm behind Silas's head and let her hand rest against it caressingly. She felt him trembling violently. He was silent for some moments when Mr. Cass had ended—powerless under the conflict of emotions, all alike painful. Eppie's heart was swelling at the sense that her father was in distress, and she was just going to lean down and speak to him when one struggling dread at last gained the mastery over every other in Silas, and he said faintly:

"Eppie, my child, speak. I won't stand in your way. Thank Mr. and Mrs. Cass."

Eppie took her hand from her father's head and came forward a step. Her cheeks were flushed, but not with shyness this time. The sense that her father was in doubt and suffering banished that sort of self-consciousness. She dropped a low curtsy, first to Mrs. Cass and then to Mr. Cass, and said—

"Thank you, ma'am—thank you, sir, but I can't leave my father nor own anybody nearer than him. And I don't want to be a lady—thank you all the same" (here Eppie dropped another curtsy). "I couldn't give up the folks I've been used to."

Eppie's lip began to tremble a little at the last words. She retreated to her father's chair again and held him round the neck while Silas, with a subdued sob, put up his hand to grasp hers.

The tears were in Nancy's eyes, but her sympathy with Eppie was, naturally, divided with distress on her

husband's account. She dared not speak, wondering what was going on in her husband's mind.

Godfrey felt an irritation inevitable to almost all of us when we encounter an unexpected obstacle. He had been full of his own penitence and resolution to retrieve his error as far as the time was left to him; he was possessed with all-important feelings that were to lead to a predetermined course of action that he had fixed on as the right, and he was not prepared to enter with lively appreciation into other people's feelings counteracting his virtuous resolves. The agitation with which he spoke again was not quite unmixed with anger.

"But I've a claim on you, Eppie—the strongest of all claims. It's my duty, Marner, to own Eppie as my child and provide for her. She's my own child; her mother was my wife. I've a natural claim on her that must stand before every other."

Eppie had given a violent start and turned quite pale. Silas, on the contrary, who had been relieved by Eppie's answer from the dread lest his mind should be in opposition to hers, felt the spirit of resistance in him set free, not without a touch of parental fierceness. "Then, sir," he answered, with an accent of bitterness that had been silent in him since the memorable day when his youthful hope had perished—"then, sir, why didn't you say so sixteen year ago, and claim her before I'd come to love her, i'stead o' coming to take her from me now, when you might as well take the heart out o' my body? God gave her to me because you turned your back upon her, and He looks upon her as mine. You've no right to her! When a man turns a blessing from his door, it falls to them as take it in."

"I know that, Marner. I was wrong. I've repented of my conduct in that matter," said Godfrey, who could not help feeling the edge of Silas's words.

"I'm glad to hear it, sir," said Marner with gathering excitement, "but repentance doesn't alter what's been going on for sixteen years. Your coming now and saying 'I'm her father' doesn't alter the feelings inside us. It's me she's been calling her father ever since she could say the word."

"But I think you might look at the thing more reasonably, Marner," said Godfrey, unexpectedly awed by the weaver's direct truth-speaking. "It isn't as if she was to be taken quite away from you so that you'd never see her again. She'll be very near you and come to see you very often. She'll feel just the same toward you."

"Just the same?" said Marner more bitterly than ever. "How'll she feel just the same for me as she does now, when we eat o' the same bit, and drink o' the same cup, and think o' the same things from one day's end to another? Just the same? That's idle talk. You'd cut us i' two."

Godfrey, unqualified by experience to discern the pregnancy of Marner's simple words, felt rather angry again. It seemed to him that the weaver was very selfish (a judgment readily passed by those who have never tested their own power of sacrifice) to oppose what was undoubtedly for Eppie's welfare, and he felt himself called upon for her sake to assert his authority.

"I should have thought, Marner," he said severely, "I should have thought your affection for Eppie would make you rejoice in what was for her good, even if it did call upon you to give up something. You ought to remember your own life's uncertain, and she's at an age now when her lot may soon be fixed in a way very different from what it would be in her father's home. She may marry some low workingman, and then, no matter what I might do for her, I couldn't make her well off. You're putting yourself in the way of her welfare; and though I'm sorry to hurt you after what you've done and what I've left undone, I feel now it's my duty to insist on taking care of my own daughter. I want to do my duty."

It would be difficult to say whether it were Silas or Eppie that was more deeply stirred by this last speech of Godfrey's. Thought had been very busy in Eppie as she listened to the contest between her old, long-loved father and this new, unfamiliar father who had suddenly

193

come to fill the place of that black, featureless shadow which had held the ring and placed it on her mother's finger. Her imagination had darted backward in conjectures, and forward in previsions, of what this revealed fatherhood implied; and there were words in Godfrey's last speech that helped to make the previsions especially definite. Not that these thoughts, either of past or future, determined her resolution—*that* was determined by the feelings which vibrated to every word Silas had uttered; but they raised, even apart from these feelings, a repulsion toward the offered lot and the newly revealed father.

Silas, on the other hand, was again stricken in conscience and alarmed lest Godfrey's accusation should be true—lest he should be raising his own will as an obstacle to Eppie's good. For many moments he was mute, struggling for the self-conquest necessary to the uttering of the difficult words. They came out tremulously.

"I'll say no more. Let it be as you will. Speak to the child. I'll hinder nothing."

Even Nancy, with all the acute sensibility of her own affections, shared her husband's view that Marner was not justifiable in his wish to retain Eppie after her real father had avowed himself. She felt that it was a very hard trial for the poor weaver, but her code allowed no question that a father by blood must have a claim above that of any foster father. Besides, Nancy, all her life used to plenteous circumstances and the privileges of "respectability," could not enter into the pleasures that early nurture and habit connect with all the little aims and efforts of the poor who are born poor. To her mind, Eppie, in being restored to her birthright, was entering on a too long withheld but unquestionable good. Hence, she heard Silas's last words with relief, and thought, as Godfrey did, that their wish was achieved.

"Eppie, my dear," said Godfrey, looking at his daughter not without some embarrassment under the sense that she was old enough to judge him, "it'll always be our wish that you should show your love and gratitude to one who's been a father to you so many years, and we shall want to help you to make him comfortable in every way. But we hope you'll come to love us as well; and though I haven't been what a father should ha' been to you all these years, I wish to do the utmost in my power for you for the rest of my life and provide for you as my only child. You'll have the best of mothers in my wife—that'll be a blessing you haven't known since you were old enough to know it."

"My dear, you'll be a treasure to me," said Nancy in her gentle voice. "We shall want for nothing when we have our daughter."

Eppie did not come forward and curtsy, as she had done before. She held Silas's hand in hers and grasped it firmly—it was a weaver's hand, with the palm and fingertips that were sensitive to such pressure—while she spoke with colder decision than before.

"Thank you, ma'am—thank you, sir, for your offers—they're very great and far above my wish. I should have no delight i' life any more if I was forced to go away from my father and knew he was sitting at home athinking of me and feeling lone. We've been used to be happy together every day, and I can't think o' no happiness without him. He says he'd nobody i' the world till I was sent to him, and he'd have nothing when I was gone. He took care of me and loved me from the first, and I'll cleave to him as long as he lives, and nobody shall ever come between him and me."

"But you must make sure, Eppie," said Silas, in a low voice. "You must make sure as you won't ever be sorry that you've made your choice to stay among poor folks and with poor clothes and things, when you might ha' had everything o' the best."

His sensitiveness on this point had increased as he listened to Eppie's words of faithful affection.

"I can never be sorry, Father," said Eppie. "I shouldn't know what to think on or to wish for with fine things about me, as I haven't been used to. And it 'ud be poor work for me to put on things, and ride in a gig, and sit in a place at church, as 'ud make those whom I'm fond of think me unfitting company for 'em. What could *I* care for then?"

Nancy looked at Godfrey with a pained, questioning glance, but his eyes were fixed on the floor where he was moving the end of his stick as if he were pondering on something absently. She thought there was a word which might perhaps come better from her lips than from his.

"What you say is natural, my dear child—it's natural you should cling to those who've brought you up," she said mildly, "but there's a duty you owe to your lawful father. There's perhaps something to be given up on more sides than one. When your father opens his home to you, I think it's right you shouldn't turn your back on it."

"I can't feel as I've got any father but one," said Eppie impetuously, while the tears gathered. "I've always thought of a little home where he'd sit i' the corner, and I should fend and do everything for him. I can't think o' no other home. I wasn't brought up to be a lady, and I can't turn my mind to it. I like the workingfolks and their victuals and their ways. And," she ended passionately, while the tears fell, "I'm promised to marry a workingman, as 'ull live with Father and help me to take care of him."

Godfrey looked up at Nancy with a flushed face and smarting, dilated eyes. This frustration of a purpose

196

toward which he had set out under, the exalted consciousness that he was about to compensate in some degree for the greatest demerit of his life, made him feel the air of the room stifling.

"Let us go," he said in an undertone.

"We won't talk of this any longer now," said Nancy, rising. "We're your well-wishers, my dear—and yours too, Marner. We shall come and see you again. It's getting late now."

In this way she covered her husband's abrupt departure, for Godfrey had gone straight to the door, unable to say more.

Nancy and Godfrey walked home under the starlight in silence. When they entered the oaken parlor, Godfrey threw himself into his chair, while Nancy laid down her bonnet and shawl and stood on the hearth near her husband, unwilling to leave him even for a few minutes and yet fearing to utter any word lest it might jar on his feelings. At last Godfrey turned his head toward her and their eyes met, dwelling in that meeting without any movement on either side. That quiet, mutual gaze of a trusting husband and wife is like the first moment of rest or refuge from a great weariness or a great danger—not to be interfered with by speech or action which would distract the sensations from the fresh enjoyment of repose.

Presently he put out his hand, and as Nancy placed hers within it, he drew her toward him, and said:

"That's ended!"

She bent to kiss him and then said as she stood by his side, "Yes, I'm afraid we must give up the hope of having her for a daughter. It wouldn't be right to want to force her to come to us against her will. We can't alter her bringing up and what's come of it."

"No," said Godfrey with a keen decisiveness of tone in contrast with his usually careless and unemphatic speech. "There's debts we can't pay like money debts, by paying extra for the years that have slipped by. While I've been putting off and putting off, the trees have been growing—it's too late now. Marner was in the right in what he said about a man's turning away a blessing from his door; it falls to somebody else. I wanted to pass for childless once, Nancy—I shall pass for childless now against my wish."

Nancy did not speak immediately, but after a little while she asked, "You won't make it known, then, about Eppie's being your daughter?"

"No. Where would be the good to anybody?—only harm. I must do what I can for her in the state of life she chooses. I must see who it is she's thinking of marrying."

"If it won't do any good to make the thing known," said Nancy, who thought she might now allow herself the relief of entertaining a feeling that she had tried to silence before. "I should be very thankful for Father and Priscilla never to be troubled with knowing what was done in the past, more than about Dunsey. It can't be helped, their knowing that."

"I shall put it in my will—I think I shall put it in my will. I shouldn't like to leave anything to be found out, like this about Dunsey," said Godfrey meditatively, "but I can't see anything but difficulties that 'ud come from telling it now. I must do what I can to make her happy in her own way. I've a notion," he added after a moment's pause, "it's Aaron Winthrop she meant she was engaged to. I remember seeing him with her and Marner going away from church."

"Well, he's very sober and industrious," said Nancy, trying to view the matter as cheerfully as possible.

Godfrey fell into thoughtfulness again. Presently he looked up at Nancy sorrowfully and said:

"She's a very pretty, nice girl, isn't she, Nancy?"

"Yes, dear, and with just your hair and eyes. I wonder it had never struck me before."

"I think she took a dislike to me at the thought of my being her father. I could see a change in her manner after that."

"She couldn't bear to think of not looking on Marner as her father," said Nancy, not wishing to confirm her husband's painful impression.

"She thinks I did wrong by her mother as well as by her. She thinks me worse than I am. But she *must* think it; she can never know all. It's part of my punishment,

Nancy, for my daughter to dislike me. I should never have got into that trouble if I'd been true to you—if I hadn't been a fool. I'd no right to expect anything but evil could come of that marriage—and when I shirked doing a father's part too."

Nancy was silent. Her spirit of rectitude would not let her try to soften the edge of what she felt to be a just compunction. He spoke again after a little while, but the tone was rather changed; there was tenderness mingled with the previous self-reproach.

"I got *you*, Nancy, in spite of all; and yet I've been grumbling and uneasy because I hadn't something else—as if I deserved it."

"You've never been wanting to me, Godfrey," said Nancy with quiet sincerity. "My only trouble would be gone if you resigned yourself to the lot that's been given us."

"Well, perhaps it isn't too late to mend a bit there. Though it *is* too late to mend some things, say what they will."

Chapter 21

The next morning, when Silas and Eppie were seated at their breakfast, he said to her—

"Eppie, there's a thing I've had on my mind to do this two year, and now the money's been brought back to us, we can do it. I've been turning it over and over in the night, and I think we'll set out tomorrow, while the fine days last. We'll leave the house and everything for your godmother to take care on, and we'll make a little bundle o' things and set out."

"Where to go, Daddy?" said Eppie in much surprise.

"To my old country—to the town where I was born—up Lantern Yard. I want to see Mr. Paston, the minister. Something may ha' come out to make 'em know I was innicent o' the robbery. Mr. Paston was a man with a deal o' light—I want to speak to him about the drawing o' the lots. And I should like to talk to him about the religion o' this countryside, for I partly think he doesn't know on it."

Eppie was very joyful, for there was the prospect not only of wonder and delight at seeing a strange country, but also of coming back to tell Aaron all about it. Aaron was so much wiser than she was about most things—it would be rather pleasant to have this little advantage over him. Mrs. Winthrop, though possessed with a dim fear of dangers attendant on so long a journey, and requiring many assurances that it would not take them out of the region of carriers' carts and slow wagons, was nevertheless well pleased that Silas should revisit his own country and find out if he had been cleared from that false accusation.

"You'd be easier in your mind for the rest o' your life, Master Marner," said Dolly—"that you would. And if there's any light to be got up the Yard as you talk

201

on, we've need of it i' this world, and I'd be glad on it myself if you could bring it back."

So on the fourth day from that time, Silas and Eppie, in their Sunday clothes, with a small bundle tied in a blue linen handkerchief, were making their way through the streets of a great manufacturing town. Silas, bewildered by the changes thirty years had brought over his native place, had stopped several persons in succession to ask them the name of this town, that he might be sure he was not under a mistake about it.

"Ask for Lantern Yard, Father—ask this gentleman with the tassels on his shoulders a-standing at the shop door. He isn't in a hurry like the rest," said Eppie in some distress at her father's bewilderment and ill-at-ease, besides, amidst the noise, the movement, and the multitude of strange, indifferent faces.

"Eh, my child, he won't know anything about it," said Silas. "Gentlefolks didn't ever go up the Yard. Perhaps somebody can tell me which is the way to Prison Street, where the jail is. I know the way out o' that as if I'd seen it yesterday."

With some difficulty, after many turnings and new inquiries, they reached Prison Street. The grim walls of the jail, the first object that answered to any image in Silas's memory, cheered him with the certitude, which no assurance of the town's name had hitherto given him, that he was in his native place.

"Ah," he said, drawing a long breath, "there's the jail, Eppie. That's just the same. I aren't afraid now. It's the third turning on the left hand from the jail doors—that's the way we must go."

"Oh, what a dark, ugly place!" said Eppie. "How it hides the sky! It's worse than the workhouse. I'm glad you don't live in this town now, Father. Is Lantern Yard like this street?"

"My precious child," said Silas, smiling, "it isn't a big street like this. I never was easy i' this street myself, but I was fond o' Lantern Yard. The shops here are all altered, I think—I can't make 'em out, but I shall know the turning because it's the third."

"Here it is," he said in a tone of satisfaction as they came to a narrow alley. "And then we must go to the left again, and then straight for'ard for a bit, up Shoe Lane; and then we shall be at the entry next to the o'erhanging window, where there's the nick in the road for the water to run. Eh, I can see it all."

"Oh, Father, I'm like as if I was stifled," said Eppie. "I couldn't ha' thought as any folks lived i' this way, so close together. How pretty Stone Pit 'ull look when we get back!"

"It looks comical to *me*, child, now—and smells bad. I can't think as it usened to smell so."

Here and there a sallow, begrimed face looked out from a gloomy doorway at the strangers and increased Eppie's uneasiness so that it was a longed-for relief when they issued from the alleys into Shoe Lane, where there was a broader strip of sky.

"Dear heart!" said Silas. "Why, there's people coming out o' the Yard as if they'd been to chapel at this time o' day—a weekday noon!"

Suddenly he started and stood still with a look of distressed amazement that alarmed Eppie. They were before an opening in front of a large factory, from which men and women were streaming for their midday meal.

"Father," said Eppie, clasping his arm, "what's the matter?"

But she had to speak again and again before Silas could answer her.

"It's gone, child," he said at last in strong agitation. "Lantern Yard's gone. It must ha' been here, because here's the house with the o'erhanging window—I know that—it's just the same; but they've made this new opening, and see that big factory! It's all gone—chapel and all."

"Come in to this little brush shop and sit down, Father—they'll let you sit down," said Eppie always on the watch lest one of her father's strange attacks should come on. "Perhaps the people can tell you all about it."

But neither from the brushmaker who had come to Shoe Lane only ten years ago, when the factory was already built, nor from any other source within his reach, could Silas learn anything of the old Lantern Yard friends, or of Mr. Paston, the minister.

"The old place is all swep' away," Silas said to Dolly Winthrop on the night of his return—"the little graveyard and everything. The old home's gone; I've no home but this now. I shall never know whether they got at the truth o' the robbery nor whether Mr. Paston could ha' given me any light about the drawing o' the lots. It's dark to me, Mrs. Winthrop, that is. I doubt it'll be dark to the last."

"Well, yes, Master Marner," said Dolly, who sat with a placid, listening face now bordered by gray hairs. "I doubt it may. It's the will o' Him above as many things should be dark to us; but there's some things as I've never felt i' the dark about, and they're mostly what comes i' the day's work. You were hard done by that once, Master Marner, and it seems as you'll never know the rights of it; but that doesn't hinder there *being* a rights, Master Marner, for all it's dark to you and me."

"No," said Silas. "No, that doesn't hinder. Since the time the child was sent to me and I've come to love her as myself, I've had light enough to trusten by; and now that she says she'll never leave me, I think I shall trusten till I die."

CONCLUSION

There was one time of the year which was held in Raveloe to be especially suitable for a wedding. It was when the great lilacs and laburnums in the old-fashioned gardens showed their golden and purple wealth above the lichen-tinted walls, and when there were calves still young enough to want bucketfuls of fragrant milk. People were not so busy then as they must become when the full cheese-making and the mowing had set in; and besides, it was a time when a light bridal dress could be worn with comfort and seen to advantage.

Happily the sunshine fell more warmly than usual on the lilac tufts the morning that Eppie was married, for her dress was a very light one. She had often thought, though with a feeling of renunciation, that the perfection of a wedding dress would be a white cotton with the tiniest pink sprig at wide intervals, so that when Mrs. Godfrey Cass begged to provide one and asked Eppie to choose what it should be, previous meditation had enabled her to give a decided answer at once.

Seen at a little distance as she walked across the churchyard and down the village, she seemed to be attired in pure white, and her hair looked like the dash of gold on a lily. One hand was on her husband's arm, and with the other she clasped the hand of her father, Silas.

"You won't be giving me away, Father," she had said before they went to church; "you'll only be taking Aaron to be a son to you."

Dolly Winthrop walked behind with her husband, and there ended the little bridal procession.

There were many eyes to look at it, and Miss Priscilla Lammeter was glad that she and her father had happened to drive up to the door of Red House just in time to see this pretty sight. They had come to keep Nancy company today, because Mr. Cass had had to go away to Lytherly, for special reasons. That seemed to be a pity, for otherwise he might have gone, as Mr. Crackenthorp and Mr. Osgood certainly would, to look on at the wedding feast that he had ordered at the Rainbow—he naturally feeling a great interest in the weaver who had been wronged by one of his own family.

"I could ha' wished Nancy had had the luck to find a child like that and bring her up," said Priscilla to her father as they sat in the gig. "I should ha' had something young to think of then, besides the lambs and the calves."

"Yes, my dear, yes," said Mr. Lammeter, "one feels that as one gets older. Things look dim to old folks; they'd need have some young eyes about 'em to let 'em know the world's the same as it used to be."

Nancy came out now to welcome her father and sister, and the wedding group had passed on beyond Red House to the humbler part of the village.

Dolly Winthrop was the first to divine that old Mr. Macey, who had been set in his armchair outside his own door, would expect some special notice as they passed, since he was too old to be at the wedding feast.

"Mr. Macey's looking for a word from us," said Dolly. "He'll be hurt if we pass him and say nothing—and him so racked with rheumatiz."

So they turned aside to shake hands with the old man. He had looked forward to the occasion and had his premeditated speech.

"Well, Master Marner," he said in a voice that quavered a good deal, "I've lived to see my words come true. I was the first to say there was no harm in you, though your looks might be again' you, and I was the first to say you'd get your money back. It's nothing but rightful as you should. I'd ha' said the 'Amens,' and willing, at the holy matrimony; but Tookey's done it a good while now, and I hope you'll have none the worse luck."

In the open yard before the Rainbow, the party of guests were already assembled, though it was still nearly an hour before the appointed feast time. But by this means they could not only enjoy the slow advent of their pleasure, they had also ample leisure to talk of Silas Marner's strange history and arrive by due degrees at the conclusion that he had brought a blessing on himself by acting like a father to a lone, motherless child. Even the farrier did not negative this sentiment.

On the contrary, he took it up as peculiarly his own and invited any hardy person present to contradict him. He met with no contradiction, and all differences among the company were merged in a general agreement with Mr. Snell's sentiment that when a man had deserved good luck, it was the part of his neighbors to wish him joy.

As the bridal group approached, a hearty cheer was raised in the Rainbow yard, and Ben Winthrop, whose jokes had retained their acceptable flavor, found it agreeable to turn in there and receive congratulations, not requiring the proposed interval of quiet at Stone Pit before joining the company.

Eppie had a larger garden than she had ever expected there now, and in other ways there had been alterations at the expense of Mr. Cass, the landlord, to suit Silas's larger family. He and Eppie had declared that they would rather stay at Stone Pit than go to any new home. The garden was fenced with stones on two sides, but in front there was an open fence, through which the flowers shone with answering gladness as the four united people came within sight of them.

"Oh, Father," said Eppie, "what a pretty home ours is! I think nobody could be happier than we are."